I0764369

MARMALADE

MARMALADE

Stories

as a basket of oranges
picked at random
to be
peeled, boiled
tasted...

by
Elizabeth Muldrow

SANTA FE

"Elevator" was first published in PITCH WEEKLY, December 21, 1995.

"Mom's Violets" was awarded Honorable Mention in the Genre Short Story Category of the 2000 WRITERS' DIGEST Writing Competition.

This is a work of fiction. Names, characters, places and incidents either are the product of the author's imagination or are used fictitiously. Any resemblance to events or persons living or dead is entirely coincidental.

Sunstone books may be purchased for educational, business, or sales promotional use. For information please write: Special Markets Department, Sunstone Press, P.O. Box 2321, Santa Fe, New Mexico 87504-2321.

Library of Congress Cataloging-in-Publication Data:

Muldrow, Elizabeth Smith, 1931-
Marmalade : stories / by Elizabeth Muldrow.
p. cm.
ISBN 0-86534-434-5
1. Southern States—Social life and customs—Fiction. I. Title.
PS3613.U43M37 2004
813'.54—dc22

2004014306

WWW.SUNSTONEPRESS.COM

SUNSTONE PRESS / POST OFFICE BOX 2321 / SANTA FE, NM 87504-2321 /USA
(505) 988-4418 / *ORDERS ONLY* (800) 243-5644 / FAX (505) 988-1025

CONTENTS

ACKNOWLEDGMENTS

My deepest appreciation to: Eric Mason who patiently edited this collection; Sarah Doyle who read "Mom's Violets" with an eye to all things adolescent; Deborah Douglas and Ann Rowe whose thoughtful insights I treasure; my husband, William, without whose loving critique I could not write; James Smith of Sunstone Press who brought the manuscript into being; and finally, but not least, the others of my supportive, often long-suffering, family and friends who read and then reread these stories during the various stages of their development. Thank you, one and all.

—Elizabeth Muldrow
Santa Fe

". . .forget the past!, . . Why? How can I?
The past is the present, isn't it?
It's the future, too.
We all try to lie out of that but life won't let us."

—Eugene O'Neill

KINFOLK

What's left of the story

She picked out pieces of the past from a thick tangle of memory, pinched fuzzies off one by one in the same persistent way she pulled at the woolly balls massed on the ragged sleeves of her sweater. Tight curls of fiber rolled on the tips of her pudgy fingers into larger and larger aggregations to be first examined, then caressed and, finally, flicked in the direction of the corner waste basket.

The hard edge of present reality annoyed her. The need to interrupt reverie for the basic routines: eating a meal, tending her toilet, finding her shoes.

At ninety-six, she alone remained, the last to have been born in the big house. The remnants of her family's records lodged with her: yellowed letters, frayed deeds, belabored wills, hurried business notations. They cluttered the tops of her tables, jumbled too close to soggy tea bags and blobs of red current jelly on her cramped kitchen counters.

She spent her best time reviewing her documents, searching the stubby ink strokes for fragments of plantation life: statements of cotton sold, inventories of supplies procured, lists of slaves owned, tallies of their worth at auction. Sometimes, bent into an overseer's faded entry, she managed to twist a number or a name into a wisp of recall. At such times her mind twirled with remembered sensation: the taste of fresh plums, the finger-scorching heat of coffee served in a tin kitchen mug, the tingle of adolescent games screened from view by the thick green foliage of the outhouse privet hedge.

Decades ago, the day they had buried her great grandmother, her mother had carried her as a four-year-old across the cotton fields to the small family cemetery. There her father supervised the two black men, diggers of every family grave since way before the war. Father had also helped shoulder the long pine box fashioned overnight for the stern matriarch who had piloted them through all the changes. Present memory focused on her tiny mother who, with no one to help bear a heavy toddler, had put her little one down. Ninety-two years later there still remained the gritty feel of warm sand sifting through her baby shoes.

Now in the blessed peace of her bed where she lay somnolent beneath the weight of treasured heavy linen sheets, long strands of memory swirled in and out of her night hours. Floatings so intense, so pleasant that, to protect them, she kept the blinds tightly drawn against the advance of daylight. In the restless slumber of early morning she could breathe each transformed moment delicately as a child puffs dandelion parachutes into the wind.

There had been the fire, after that the Depression, followed by financial collapse and the forced sale of the land. And after that, the Diaspora. For her, the departure had meant a respectable, if low paid, position as a secretary in Chicago. For decades she had lived alone in the city, three rickety flights up. Week after week she had walked the ten blocks to the office, five each Sunday to church. The escapes into the past began then, to fill the long gray gaps in her days. Finally, a potent tug of retrospection brought her back to home country. Overnight, on the bus with one suitcase and the great trunk filled with family papers.

Once there, the social service office had provided her with a tiny apartment. A nice girl named Anna Virginia dropped by weekly to see about things. Anna Virginia understood her elderly client's need for sleep. When one of the Venetian blinds twisted in its cord permitting beams of early morning sun to interrupt her slumber, Anna Virginia had seen to it that Big Joe came over to set things right.

That's how she'd gotten to know Big Joe. He had told her about the two old black men who'd dug the graves since way before The War. She liked to talk to Big Joe. They discussed the burials out beyond the cotton field and her faint memory of the men who'd shoveled first the rich brown humus beneath the trees and then the deeper bronzed alluvial sand into a heap at the side of the deep hole.

"They'd be my Pa's Pa and his brother, I'm thinkin'," Big Joe had told her.

Big Joe always went on about things, but he was very conscientious. And when he had finished fixing the blind he'd put everything back precisely so. She had supervised from the comfort of the great wicker rocker, but really it hadn't been necessary. Big Joe treated her papers with care. He had a great interest, he told her, in kinfolk.

She'd made coffee. They sat in the kitchen, she on her straight chair while he settled himself on the stoop, propping open the screen door with his back.

He took his coffee black, in a mug. She took hers in the last of Grandmother's pink flowered Haviland cups, added sugar and a tap of milk, skim because the doctor had told her to cut down on fat. Not that it would do any good. She had thrown out her scales years ago. When the Good Lord got around to it, he'd take her no matter what shape she happened to be in at the time. Too much interference would only serve to delay the Lord's visit. Who would want to do that to the Almighty? So she added a tablespoonful of whiskey to the coffee in her pink flowered china cup.

"Sure thing, nothin' at all," Big Joe agreed and smiled as she slipped in another measure, this from the whiskey bottle itself.

"For my heart," she told him.

He nodded and they talked about her work, the time it took to sort through more than two centuries worth of crumbling record. To weight the piles she used small rocks picked up along the edge of the road. He promised to bring her some smooth river stones when he came by again.

"What," Big Joe wanted to know, "you learn'n from all this study, Miss Lilly?"

"It's a reunion, like a getting together of kin," she replied.

They talked about the plantation. How it had been nothing but wolves and rattlesnakes when living souls first put foot in the wilderness three hundred years ago. How everybody lived in the dirt of log shacks while they cleared the fields and how, finally, things had become easier so they could build the big house. The grand one with verandahs all around, set high up on brick piers so that fancy folk in pretty carriages could make a dry entrance even in bad weather.

He nodded in rhythm with her tale. "My grandpappy told me all 'bout that," he said.

"About the house?" Her glasses slid to the end of her nose.

He nodded, wrapped both hands around his mug, took a careful sip. "My grandmammy's daddy lived all his life there," he said. "Told lots of stories about those times. I never knew him much except as old and bent and sittin' and rockin' all day by the stove. But he could recall good. We'd get him warmed up with a couple shots of corn liquor and a hot fire, and he'd set out down the memory path just as steady as a hound's nose leading to bobcat."

He told her what he had heard about how the big house came to be made so many years ago. About the master's walking about measuring and having folks set out stakes in the ground just so, and how the mistress moved the stakes because of the view from her bedroom. And how each brick maker marked his bricks with a personal sign so ever after his kin would know how he had been part of the building. And how those who went out to fell cedar for the walls and pine for the floors did the same, chiseling their marks into the lengths of board. He drew his mammy's daddy's, and his own daddy's X on the wood below her screen door's handle.

With her third finger she traced an X across the Formica of her kitchen table. For her the writing pulled up into memory the scent of wide cedar planks. The kitchen wall. The corner behind the wood stove where the planks butted against the old fireplace. The builders' marks on the butt ends of thick planks, and on the bricks. The old hearth which, in her childhood, had sheltered a great iron cook stove.

The strong aroma of coffee kept always hot on the back of that stove came to her. Coffee kept so for her father. Cook would pour his tin cup full, wrap it in a cloth so as not to burn the fingers of the child who would carry the coffee, one careful step at a time, to where he sat covered in field dust on the edge of the porch. She closed her eyes and found it all right there. Even the taste of the coffee.

The fire that ended it all started in the kitchen flue, Big Joe told her. At first it was nothing, the kitchen separate and all. The cook called to the stable man who came running with the yard boy. They beat it out right quick and went back to their business. But after dark the wind picked up one small spark and, puff, the house roof just blew up in flame.

By then Big Joe's mother had moved him, her first son, over to a shack near the main road and she'd married, so there were two more little ones, his half brothers, who crawled about on the dirt floor and whose toes tickled his nose at night when they shared his corn husk mattress. Big Joe remembered his new father running off to fight the blaze. And how, on the man's return later that night, the kerosene lantern his mother kept on the dresser had lighted the tear marks dried onto his soot smeared cheeks.

"The marks. They's all gone," he'd heard his stepfather say.

"Like if you was to lose your papers," Big Joe told her.

Must have been an hour they'd sat there that day, she by the table, he on the stoop, the sun dipping lower over the cotton. They'd snatched at those memories like someone snipping at the tight stitches in a worn garment. Not easy, unraveling the long bobbin thread of the past.

It came to her that night. They could go to the house. His pickup could easily clear the old road's high crown, maybe even plow through the marsh beyond the branch.

"No track left after the branch," he told her the next day, and "I don't think much, Miss Lilly, of you trying to walk the distance. Varmints and such like have had the place to themselves for too long now. But, I'll see." With that he got up from the stoop, walked briskly to his truck. He pulled sharp into the right hand turn at the end of her drive, tapped his horn in leaving.

Getting her up into the passenger side of the pickup proved effort enough. His son's youngest, Little Joe, came over to help. One of them to each side of her. The boy rode between straw bales in the truck bed. She offered him peppermints through the window above the seat back.

Little Joe looked away, shyly turned his eyes down when she said, "Here, boy, take some of these."

"Nice boy. Polite," she said to Big Joe who nodded.

The sun profiled Big Joe's long straight nose, the determined set to his jaw. Big Joe reminded her somehow of the Theisen family. That square set of the jaw, the long taper of the nose. Like Cousin Billy Theisen. Discomforting, that thought. She waved the idea away with the fly that persisted in alighting on her peppermints.

Twenty peppermints had filled the bag to begin with. By the time they turned off the road onto a single sand track, only three remained for the return trip. She'd already given Little Joe five. She smiled at the memory of her mother's voice demanding, as mother always had, a precise count of sugar candies as well as silver spoons.

At first the track moved easily along the edge of the field. Soybeans. Then trees, scrub cedar, some oak with long strings of moss.

"The oaks," Big Joe said, "were planted along the road to the house. They didn't grow naturally. Old Master made a long road to the house," he told her, "so everyone would know company's coming and have time to get into proper clothes to greet the visitor."

Big Joe kept his eyes fixed on the track ahead, his hands engaged in steering around branches downed in the last storm. She ran a finger over the chrome on his dash, all the while wondering why nothing on the road moved her imagination. Only the peppermints.

Then the dark tannin smell of her many childhood romps among the tree limbs came to her. She thought of Billy Theisen who'd kissed her and run his hand up her braless back while they sat thigh to thigh between the branches. She had liked his explorations until he told her he'd learned to do the deep tongue trick from Vini Mae, the black cook's well rounded daughter who'd taught it to all the boys.

She'd called Billy dirty. Stuck her fingers in her ears.

She glanced sideways at Big Joe. "Is your mother's name Vini Mae?"

"Sure enough," he grinned.

He favored his mother except in the long taper of the nose and the square line of the jaw. Resisting the recognition that wanted to slither its way up from deep inside her, she unscrewed the cap on her water bottle and took a long drowning swig.

The track narrowed even more. Blackberry runners filled the ditches on either side. Blackberry runners. One of those threads of memory reminded her of long tears in a little girl's dress. Vini Mae, barely older than she, but already skilled in household deceptions, had once attempted to mend a rend with thread snitched from the mistress' sewing basket.

As Big Joe had thought, they couldn't go beyond the branch in the pickup. She wouldn't be able to see the ruins. On foot the boy and his grandfather pushed through the marsh tangle and up to the top of the rise. Returning with bricks from the chimneys, they showed her the maker's marks, the X's and the others.

"All grown over," they told her. "Home to snakes. The plums've gone wild, but still in rows so you can trace out the orchard. They's not ripe yet, Miss Lilly, or we'd brought you some."

She closed her eyes, ran memory's tongue slowly across cornbread layered in deep purple jam, sucked the leavings from the preserve kettle off her fingers.

"Maybe we could have Pris make you up something when they's ripe," they told her.

Later that summer she got the idea from Pris's plum butter. Big Joe'd brought over a quart jar full.

"There's more," he told her as he checked one of the back burners on her stove.

"You need to take care, Miss Lilly. Got to clean these foil liners when your soup boils over. That's what's smoking. Could get you some trouble."

He brought in a couple of smooth river stones to weight down the papers she'd stacked on the narrow kitchen counter.

"You know," he said, "these papers go and there'll be no record at all, except maybe on those stones in that burial plot of your'n."

Right then the thought floated in like a red bird swooping down to perch on the gardenia by her doorstep. She had to go at once.

Big Joe said he'd drive her out to the burial place, but he'd have to leave her for a while to take care of some business in town. He'd be back in an hour or so. She could sit by the road in the shade of the huge magnolia while she waited.

At the turn-off by the magnolia he brushed clean a stump, swept some of the tree trash from around where she'd put her feet, gave her his plastic bottle of water just in case she caught a thirst in all the heat.

"You sure you gonna be all right?" He asked.

The long wisps of memory didn't begin to stream together in her mind until she'd taken a few steps beyond the hard clay path. In the turned soil of the cotton field her feet sank into the sand up to the tops of her unlaced oxfords. The roll of her ample stomach made panting work of reaching down to tie her shoes. She remembered too late the need to refill her prescription for nitroglycerin.

She put up her best umbrella. Its yellow roses flounced in the heat. The warm sand sifted between her heel and the loose back of her shoe. Father's Chinaberry trees waved at her from across the field. She wanted to run toward them, but the sand hindered her steps. The rhythm of her footfalls reached deep into herself.

She glimpsed the first gravestone before she'd even entered the shade. The marker, yes indeed, that's Aunt Molly's little one, Peter.

"Hello Peter. Sweet thing."

A break in the trees gave her entrance. She swatted the vines aside with the umbrella, then, stepping beyond the line of sunlight, propped its ruffles up against a trunk.

"And yes, here you are, sweet Maggie, so young to have passed as you did. How nice to have you all out here playing together. We'll have lemonade at four."

Waving adieu to the children she bent over to examine the larger stones.

Aunt Emily. The typhoid took her. As she brushed aside the cover of leaves, the hushed solemnity of a darkened house and the haste with which her father had escorted her out the rear hall door came tumbling back. The cold dread of contagion. The ebon pleat of her mother's veil. The precise line of her mother's shoe tips set in this very depression where her's now fit.

"Seventeen." She told herself out loud. "I was seventeen."

And at that graveside Cousin Billy began making sideways eyes at her through the sheaf of long blond hair tumbling across his face. He had leaned against the old tree, pushed his hair back and smiled an invitation into his wider world of military school and lipsticked debs. She turned abruptly to avoid remembering the breaking hurt after they'd had each other behind the screen of privet two nights later. He'd left for France. She'd learned shortly thereafter about Vini Mae's baby.

Billy hadn't come home from France.

The leaves overhead filtered the light. Pleasant. She sat down on a log. A little breeze fanned the perspiration running in rivulets from her forehead, dampening her bosom. She remembered the water bottle she'd left at the spot under the magnolia tree, moved one foot to trap some of the breeze between her legs. Her shoe caught on a stone. Picking up a stick she brushed aside the woody accumulation of debris to reveal part of a small stone, a foot marker inscribed A.S. Her mother.

"Dear mother, I'm back for a visit."

She thought of plum butter, of blackberry cobbler, of lumps of sugar candy hidden under her pillow, and of ladies working their intricate stitches on lacy hankies, and of a mother's tiny fingers soothing the knots in a daughter's back after the news about Verdun. She touched the chain around her neck. Her mother's rings. Too tiny for her own thick fingers. In a silent convulsion of pain she knelt over the depression by the small stone marked A.S. She had helped her father smooth the earth with his bare hands. She looked for the rose he had planted, the dear pink one mother so loved, but the rose had gone in a longing for full sun. With a stick she dug for the headstone. She scraped. The stick frayed in her hands. She scratched. Her nails became scoops congested with dirt. They rasped across the buried marble slab.

"I'm coming," she called. "I'll be right there. Yes, I'm hurrying. Yes, I'm dressed, but I still have to pin up my hair. Yes, let's go in the Rambler with the top down, we'll feel the cool breeze on our faces. Be sure to pack some of the preserves in the picnic basket, and a jug of water too."

It took all of them, Big Joe, and Little Joe and the farmer who owned the cotton field, to lift her into the back of Joe's pickup. They didn't have a blanket, so Little Joe rode beside her holding the umbrella with the yellow roses to shield her face from the sun. She looked so happy that Big Joe debated about closing her eyelids, but then he decided he'd better shut them out of respect. Just the same, she smiled the whole way back into town. The undertaker rubbed his hand across his clean-shaven chin a few times, but then left her beaming up on all who came to call.

"Must be greetin' a whole bunch of kinfolk," he told those gathered in his parlor.

Big Joe came to the service. Sat to the rear, kept his hat in hand. He thought about their sharing of coffee, and plum butter, and the burning of the house, and their family graves out beneath the Chinaberry trees in the middle of the cotton field.

And he thought about how Miss Anna Virginia at social services had called to say she wanted all that mess in Miss Lilly's place cleaned out right quick.

She'd asked him if there was much in all those papers.

"The record," he'd told her, "what's left of the story."

MARMALADE

Revisions in sweet bits and twisted peel

All day on the drive into Carolina the old tale has frothed in and out of mind, a sweet tidbit surfacing here, a curl of twisted peel there. Settled into a country inn in what was once an old plantation, I walk in the heat of late afternoon down a dirt road past an ancient cemetery. A moist breeze plasters my hair to my skull. How is it that here in the low country the dead come alive? I feel them circle around me under a rising sliver of moon.

Later over tea in a graceful parlor my hostess' cup dances about its saucer. She hooks a protective finger through the golden curve of its handle. In the final glow of evening her diamonds flash red and yellow. Glancing at the portrait above the mantel, she begins a story of terror once deemed too raw for public discourse.

"Buried in haste," she whispers. "The husband, driven mad."

Bound to an ascribed formula by the weight of both time and taste, her tale lurches forward. An infant's bones. A woman's twisted skeleton. She murmurs of bodies interred together before sundown, of the dreadful heat of late summer, the deep waters of the flood. And of his grief: terrible, crazed far beyond reason. Behind the story I hear generations mourning the imagined grace of an idyllic world long since torn beyond repair.

"The risk," she sighs, "the enormous risk attendant on any childbirth, and this one far out of the city, where, even in those long-ago days a doctor might have been procured."

I suggest that doctor's orders might well have sent the expectant mother up river to this country house set high in the pines away from the virulent fevers of the low-lying port where sea water laps at the dainty shoes of fashionable promenaders.

My hostess nods.

Our conversation shifts from the macabre to the lighter rituals of high style. We agree that city fashion would have dictated low curved heels on the shoes, an elegant bow on the instep. And roses in her hair. And ribbons blowing in the soft breeze from the sea. To shield from the sun, a parasol flipped in the manner of a coquette, the very coquette who gazes directly down at us now from within the confines of her gilded frame. Tiny rosebuds outline a firm bun. Blond hair, hazel eyes, oval face. Poised. Alert. Seated forward as if about to rise from her chair.

My hostess smiles.

"He adored her," she says.

And I hear in her speech the expectation that a husband will faithfully adore his wife, that grief over her sudden demise should be as wild as the memory of it stored so carefully alongside the dates charted precisely in the Bible of family history. Yes, it is indeed a lovely portrait. Who would not weep at the tragedy enshrined with the tale?

However, the story as told to the rhythm of silver teaspoons, lump sugar and great-grandmother's Haviland has lost the keen heart of it, the warm flesh of detail. The first routines of preparation for confinement: linens bleached and laid out, the birthing bed ticked tightly with new straw. A cradle for the wee one. A bucket. A kettle on the fire. A midwife engaged.

Our-Lady-of-Roses-in-her-Hair feels the initial pain of birth in a country garden while she gathers mint. This is not her first delivery; so she snips off the mint tops, ties them together with a pink ribbon from her hair. At her order a slave child skips off with the bouquet to the kitchen with a request for tea that afternoon. For by afternoon Our Lady, the new babe nestled beside her, will need the quiet renewal of warm tea.

A second pain grips her as she enters the house. Sharp, promising a quick time. Her other confinements, two of them, had not been long. Her mother reads her face. They say nothing, but the older woman sends for the midwife, thus alerting the household. The young mother to be retires to her room on the second floor, a chamber overlooking the river with long windows to capture the breeze. From there the tragedy unfolds.

Two and a half centuries later, I learn of this birthing in a whisper, woman to woman. Why the whisper? Is there something that might soil the white cloths prepared for the delivery? I stir lingering sugar crystals round and round in my cup, break open my biscuit and spread it thick with marmalade.

The elements of this tale gradually take hold, one word after another, much as the essence of orange bleeds from the rind during the making of marmalade, bits and pieces of ripe orange slowly coloring the liquid, creating a spread fit for the most delicate of tea cakes. A long, patient process, the making of marmalade. The parlor fire crackles. Conversation halts at the long bay of a neighbor dog hounding a rabbit through the dank undergrowth on the far edge of the velvet lawn.

Perhaps my impatient twenty-first century curiosity prevents me from pulling the fragments of this tale into a whole. I haven't allowed the words the time needed to ripen in the salt brine.

Presently, I bid my hostess good-night. She presses my hand. Her diamonds cut into my flesh.

The next morning I purchase three postcards at K-Mart: one of the old plantation house now the inn of last evening's narrative, one of the old church by which I am told she is buried, and one of Our-Lady-with-Roses-in-her-Hair, my young friend of the elegant portrait. It startles me to find her at K-Mart, smiling at me from the revolving metal rack by the cashier's stand. So out of context. How am I to slot K-Mart among the bits and pieces I've collected? How to make a fully ripened recital of it all?

The checkout girl shrugs when I show her the postcards.

I ask, "Where is this church?"

"No idea. Pretty girl," she says. "Old-fashioned."

"Yes," I reply and smile politely.

If I tell her I am looking for this girl, she will say, "Oh," tap her shiny black nails, maybe laugh through her uneven yellow teeth framed in deep purple lipstick. So I walk out toward my car, three postcards in hand. Somewhere on the other side of the parking lot's asphalt and the highway's brilliant yellow markers there stands, has stood for many years, a pink church done up with fat baroque cherubs over its windows. Somewhere thereabout, a brick tomb holds the remains of a pretty old-fashioned lady with roses in her hair, and tossed beside her the small bones of her babe. In the traditional accounting I have so recently heard, the inside of their casket is said to bear a mystery sealed off in the dark from a husband who wept prostrate above.

A discreet sign points me down a short drive along a sandy side road into a pine forest clearing. I have come on Sunday morning, but no rector reads the lesson in this lonely candy box of a building set behind an old iron gate. Beyond the gate, eroded marble headstones circle a wide lawn. Directly opposite the sanctuary door, Our Lady's tomb reigns majestically over the lesser monuments.

This sepulcher of hers is a lichen-covered rectangle of crumbling red brick set high on a heavy platform of deteriorating masonry. The bricks sealing off one end of the casket's narrow upper chamber are yellow, hard-fired, more closely mortared than their soft red counterparts.

It is clear that someone, sometime, has opened the upper chamber. Someone, sometime, has wrenched her casket from its close confinement and pried open her box. Why? And why, when the coffin was finally forced back into its narrow home, was the mason so careful, the brick so hard? Who could have dared? Foul play?

In this spot, grief hangs suspended in a fine misting of rain blown on the forward edge of a storm. The forest bends in the rising wind. The pines sigh. Beads of water wisp downward from their branches. Time collapses into this one place, into this singular tragedy. Hecate herself lurks in the gloom beyond the clearing.

My jacket clutched close against the damp, I begin the invention of a richer narrative. I undertake to boil and re-boil the tale as do the brewers of marmalade. In this first re-telling there would be the husband, absent on business in Charles Town, the young city by the sea. No matter this absence of his, for the birth is not expected for well over a month. He has kissed his wife good-bye and tousled the curls of their toddlers with a promise of speedy return. The trip, after all, is but a river cruise of four hours down to the wharves lining the busy port. His sails are good, his men expert with the ways of water, and he will return with a trinket for her and perhaps some sweets for the children. Her mother remains with her, the servants, the children. All will be well.

It is asserted that, in keeping with all fine husbands, he was young and vigorous, a good manager of his property, and in love with his pretty wife. But, he has been excluded from her bed for more than a month now and, as is so often the way with men, the fever is upon him. Accordingly, he will make arrangements for the young black girl, at the pull of his bell cord, to trip up the rear stairs of his elegant city establishment. Two nights in her warmth will suffice for now. Such an indelicacy is seldom discussed among ladies, a conspiracy his wife or her mother, would hardly acknowledge. However, had he looked up from the mound of freshly boiled shrimp on his plate that last night they dined together he would have caught a warning in the careful raising of his mother-in-law's finger when he announced his need to be gone.

But I am not satisfied. Is there yet another layer to the story, one sticking with the scrapings to the hot bottom of the kettle? One, perhaps, of an angry slave woman who deeply resents the treatment of her fourteen-year-old sister who lives in the Charles Town house?

Perhaps as we engage this third retelling of the tale, Our-Lady-with-Roses-in-her-Hair gives birth attended by her mother and the household servants. The babe is stillborn. An embittered slave woman offers the cup of hot mint tea. Soon after, Our Lady appears dead. A hasty burial takes place in her garden before sundown. Word is sent to the husband who returns up river as speedily as may be. He orders the brick platform's construction, demands to see the body. The casket's lid is found slightly askew. He screams at the sight of his beloved. Servants drag him away.

The entire event, like the casket, is promptly sealed. Only the acceptable facts, her beauty, the design of her tomb, and the frenzied agony of a loving husband's grief are deemed worthy of record. The remainder is permitted to dissolve in time, much as the studied stirring of a silver spoon fuses lump sugar into warm tea, leaving only leaves crushed in the dregs of memory.

But, again, shall we end here? Is there not a scraping left from which to create a fourth, even richer, version of the event? A retelling in which the listener cowers before a wind that roars with hell's vengeance out of the Floridas, and rain that sheets off the roofs of the slave cabins, pours from the downspouts at the big house? Our elaboration of the tale must now tell of the long-ago flood that made impassable the sand tracks between plantations, that brought the sea up over the embankments in Charles Town and into the streets, filling the lower levels with salt water and floating fancy city furniture off with the tide. And of the bloated animal carcasses bobbing in the back waters of an alley where presently they fouled the air for three blocks around.

In this enrichment of the story, the husband is delayed by the storm. By lantern's glow he must superintend the shuttering of the windows, the boarding of the openings to lower floors, the movement of supplies up narrow stairs to dry storage, and the gathering of shivering slaves from sodden quarters out back to the dry, if cold, upper floors of the main house. The overflowing of the latrines contaminating all the drinking water. The bundling together of master and servants through the long night hours of howling and crashing and roaring of waves. And the silent, dark, insistent surge of the tide as it rises higher and higher till it licks at the thick pine planks of the floor they crouch upon.

Finally, with the dawn comes a heavy calm. There is no news from the plantation, but none is expected. The roads are impassable. Trees, ancient giants, toppled like matchsticks in the ferocity of the storm, block all avenues west of the town.

The husband delays even more, to aid in setting the town to rights after the holocaust of the night. His people carry food and dry firewood, and warm clothing to those in need. He instructs the housekeeper to provide thick soup and bread for the hungry. He is, after all, a responsible man, one with an eye on the governor's appointment. Charity becomes his portfolio.

He suspends his return even longer to assist with the clearing of the roads, orders his men to cut a path through the downed trees to the governor's house. Later, with apologies for the mud on his shoes, the splatters on his leather riding britches, and the circumstances which have left his powdered wig on the top shelf of his wardrobe, he lingers for a warm brandy with the governor himself. The governor, whose gout suffers double indignity in the infernal damp of the low country, refills his guest's snifter of brandy. His ambitious young friend has performed a splendid public service on the colony's behalf. Finally, long after day's end when the young husband returns to his townhouse, a single jerk of the bell rope ensures that his bed is not lonely that night.

And what of the wife *enceinte* up country with two little ones pulling at her skirts and the heaviness of late pregnancy bearing her down as the monster storm drives in from the sea?

The storm gains steadily. The wife orders the shutters drawn, the openings sealed in the lower part of the house that, by design, sits on a rise well above the river with no fear of flood. But the driving pelts of rain force water through the tiniest of cracks and, rivering in torrents off the slates of the roof, quickly fill the cisterns to overflowing. Her mother is there to see to the toddlers and their nurse. The overseer, unwilling to track thick red mud into the house, calls up the wide stairwell to his mistress that he has checked the ditches draining the fields. All is secure.

The cook brings fresh bread and soup in a small copper kettle, hangs it to warm on the metal armature which swings over the fire flaming on our lady's hearth. The mother fetches deep bowls and spoons. The children's supper over, the nurse wipes the crumbs from the table and takes the sleepyheads off to their room for the night.

Alone together the mother chides the daughter for, unladylike, dipping the bread into her soup. With a slight shrug of apology Our Lady dozes off in a high wing chair by the hearth, her feet in tiny silken slippers propped on a small footstool. Presently, the nurse brings in the long-handled bed warmer, fills it with coals from the hearth, runs it over the sheets, assists her mistress as she removes her dressing gown. This slave wears her bondage like a dark shawl half pulled over her face, revealing only the smoldering charcoal of her eyes. She is the elder sister of the fourteen-year-old in town.

Our Lady and her mother retire for the night Sheltered against the ragings without, they huddle in the high bed. Its curtains sway in the draft. The wind howls across the roof. Slates crack and rasp as they tear loose to become lethal missiles flying with the Furies, parallel to the earth.

The two women, snug in their warm bed, pull the covers closer over their heads, but the banging and the roar outside sweep sleep away. The toddlers fret. Their sullen nurse brings them to their mother who admits them into bed beside her. They all curl together under the counterpane, sheltered from the wrath outside.

Finally, with the storm's eye, comes a lull. All but the young mistress are asleep. She who is great with child rests, as is customary, propped up by two hard bolsters, cushioned in the deep comfort of pillows filled with goose down, and covered in trousseau linen edged with her mother's tatting. She is awake when the first intimation of birth seizes her. At first she turns slightly, adjusts her sleeping children and moves her legs which have begun to cramp. By dawn, with the passage of the storm, the distress of her contractions reaches beyond pretense. She arouses her mother and sends for the children's nurse who is also skilled in midwifery.

Word spreads in concentric circles through the line of cabins, across the sodden fields. The overseer posts a rider to take word to the husband lingering in town.

The women gather in the bedroom of the mistress: the mother, the household's cook and the nurse/midwife, who is the sullen charcoal-eyed elder sister of the fourteen-year-old in the town. Working together they strip the bed of its fine linen and make it up with the courser pieces of muslin bleached in preparation for this hour. As they work the mistress sits in her chair by the fire or, with one of the women by her side, walks to and from the door to the windows still shuttered tightly against the night's alarms. Her back pains now dull but pressing, she sits again and then moans into a faint. The women carry her to her bed. She awakens. Bites her lip into a sharp red line over a scream. Strains against the rope now attached to the headboard. At mid-afternoon the midwife of the smoldering charcoal eyes delivers a stillborn child. She stumbles as she carries off the soiled linens and a half bucket of her lady's blood. Hands shaking she prepares a cup of hot, mint scented tea for her mistress' lips. A sip and Our-Lady-of-Roses-in-her-Hair drops off to sleep. An hour later they cannot find her pulse.

Her mother sends for the overseer who orders the pine coffin. He dispatches two slaves to speed swiftly over water for the husband and then calls for two more hands to dig the grave.

But the grave diggers return to tell him of water that, rising in the night, has so soaked the earth that no deep, dry hole may be dug. Accordingly, he arranges for a temporary resting place by the side of her high garden wall, the very same garden where Our Lady gathered herbs only the day before.

By the failing light at the end of the day, they carry the pine coffin down the wide stair and out the finely carved door. The entire plantation has gathered, the field hands, the household help, even the sullen nurse who is the elder sister of the young girl in town. This sister-in-bondage pulls her black shawl tight across her face so that none can see the smirk flitting at the edges of her mouth. The others, fearing the blaze visible in her charcoal eyes, stand well apart.

By noon the next day the neighbors begin to arrive. Over muddy tracks, through thickets of downed trees, by water over waves still settling from their violent churning of one full night ago. Two nights later he is there. He must see her, inside her pine box. Her mother, his friends dissuade. They point to her portrait over his great room mantle.

"Remember this," they urge him.

He appears to agree and in the morning begins in a frenzy the brick platform in the yard of the pink church. At its completion laborers remove her pine box from the garden and close it into its final chamber. That night, eluding his household, the husband stumbles off, makes his way to her tomb, yanks out an end section of soft red brick and pries open her casket. By wavering lantern flame it is he who finds the marks of her fingernails, her dress twisted, the babe tossed to the side. The overseer hears his scream, finds him with the body of Our Lady in his arms. With the help of servants he is dragged away. The casket is replaced and the narrow opening firmly secured with hard yellow brick leaving time to trickle this terrible tale into memory.

These then are the whisperings, peelings ripened into a tart spread for the teacakes presented on antique silver trays to the old plantation's twenty-first century guests who silently observe Our Lady's portrait as they contemplate morsels too bitter-sweet for easy recollection.

COOKIES

The determined child

Reader, attend, as the tall parlor clock in an antiseptic home for the elderly strikes the hour of midnight. One floor up, at the far end of a long corridor, a blue light flickers from beneath the door of room 224.

Enter room 224. Find there an elderly woman rocking mechanically back and forth, back and forth in an antique oaken chair. Her fingers clutch the chair's arms precisely where the brass upholstery tacks meet the hard turn of the wood. Her eyes rivet the TV screen, but they see another time. For this ancient resident of room 224, life strains between an unfinished past and the institutional reality of her present.

In her long ago past not a breath of air stirs the lace sheers pulled back to the edge of an open window.

By the window a little girl sits on the edge of a small oak rocker. Dark curls, damp with the heat, frame her face. Her hands clasp the rounded edges of the rocker's handrails so tightly that their nails show white. With great care she positions her shoes so that their tips meet exactly.

On the top of a massive traditional dresser a lady from long ago stares into space from her tarnished tin frame. A beaten gold bowknot nestles in the ruffle at the base of the patrician neck. Seated beneath her mother's picture The Old Woman strokes the self-same gold bowknot clinging unsteadily to the light fabric of her bodice. Quite properly, her afternoon dress is of dimity, a fabric too light for the burdensome weight of the gold.

A slight movement at the door shifts The Child's attention. A woman enters. The Child, leaping out of her chair, stands bolt upright beside it.

"Comb your hair. Straighten your dress. Mind your shoes."

The woman's words lash at The Child, who flinches before moving mechanically to the dresser. She picks up a brush to push at the tangles tumbled about her forehead. With a shake, she attends to her frock. A quick glance at her mother's unyielding back, and she dares to rub the dust from her shoe tips off onto the carpet. Her toilet complete, the Child escapes into the hall. There she pauses by a great dark door, one framed so precisely that not a glimmer of light slips through. Cautiously, The Child taps on the dark wood of the door. At a sound from within, she enters.

The walls of her room are painted a sterile white. Her bed is of hard steel tubes. A heavy door, cut wide to accommodate hospital gurneys, provides access to the hall. The Old Woman stumbles as she moves toward the hall door. Her cane pokes at its metal frame, but it's the wrong door. She returns slowly, unsteadily, to the worn comfort of the antique rocker.

The masters of old southern houses passed their nights in large, high beds with dark rosewood posts rounded on a craftsman's spinning lathe into the shape of cannon balls. The Child's father lies on such a bed. To ease his shallow breathing, a small pillow of hard, packed straw holds up his head. The dryness of his deathly yellow skin pulls his mouth taut. Above sharp cheeks the eyes bulge several sizes too large. Death pauses momentarily beyond the long lace sheers hung in the narrow bay of the window waiting for the father to bid farewell to his child. When The Child approaches the high bed, a slight movement of the middle finger of the man's right hand motions her toward his final gift, a token guarded within the drawer of a bedside table of brown-stained country pine.

"My child." The dying voice rasps with the noise of a knife being sharpened. Slowly, in the manner of a mechanical figure, The Child's left hand reaches out to the drawer, pulls from its depth a large sugar cookie. She slips the cookie into the pocket of her cotton pinafore.

The mother enters to stand watch at the foot of the bed. Her hand fingers a bowknot nestled in the silk ruching gathered about her throat. Its gold, offering both frozen respectability and protection from emotion's warmer arrows, armors the patrician for battle.

"Go. Ask Cook how you are to help. Keep your shoes clean." The mother's sharp whisper pistols through the space between them.

The Child turns and walks slowly from the room with its high bed, down the hall with its dark corners, down the back stairs with their high narrow risers, across the verandah with its imperfect shade, and into the garden patch with its tall stakes of pole beans. Hidden there she reaches into her pocket for the cookie.

"You come here, Miss. Set the table." Cook's voice speeding from the kitchen invades the little one's shelter beneath the tall pole beans.

Obediently, The Child precisely places the forks and then the knives about the dining room table. She sets three places, one here for her mother, another over there for herself, and yet another at the head for her father. (She pauses momentarily to consider the place for her father.) Finding a strip of old linen with which to polish the spoons, she holds one up, this way to see herself upside down, that way to look long and pinched in the middle. She sticks her tongue out at herself. It too looks long and pinched in the middle.

"Miss, get some flowers for the center. Salve for the heart, Miss."

The Child, taking the proffered knife and the small basket, makes her way out a side door to where a company of gaudy phlox waves boldly against the worn, white clapboard of the kitchen. After piling several flower tops into the basket, she turns back toward the kitchen. Depositing her basket on the edge of the verandah, she finds a low blue bowl and, vessel in hand, runs to fill it at the hand pump by the walk to the woodshed.

The TV announcer spouts a tenth repeat of the day's news. The Old Woman appears to listen. At the conclusion of the newscast, she adjusts her dress and searches yet again for the right door, the one to the bathroom. For her it is a long journey to the bathroom. One always bathes before bedtime, but the advance of old age has made the process more difficult.

With determined poking about, the bathroom is found. She pauses by the tub, cautious of its uncertain depth, and its hard white invitation to a fall. With a sigh of resignation she turns to the basin. Earlier in the day an aide had turned the spigots tight. The Old Woman's trembling fingers pry at the taps until, finally, the cold yields. She sponges in the cold water.

The Child pumps vigorously to prime the pipe. Finally the stream runs cool and strong. The water, splashing over her pinafore front, soaks what remains of the pocketed cookie. Hastily, she scoops out the soggy mess and flings it away. Food for the birds.

The bowl that The Child has placed beneath the pump's mouth overflows. She tips some out. Even then, as she retrieves the basket, the water sloshes into her shoes, leaves tracks on the painted pattern of the dining room's stiff canvas floor cover. Standing by the table she mounds the phlox heads at the center of the blue bowl. One tumbles to the cloth where it half hides an ugly scorch mark.

The mother's bulk fills the doorway. Again her orders pistol across the space. "Go to the kitchen by the porch, not through the room. Mind you don't set your shoes too near the heat." The short, sharp, tone of the voice scrapes at The Child.

The painted floor canvas must be mopped at once for it shows each step in the parade of young footprints. An negligence hardly befitting the formalities of the noon meal.

The Old Woman had not bothered to lace her shoes this morning, two rows of eyelets, five on each row, black on black. She can barely distinguish between them in full daylight, certainly not in the glow from the TV across the room. Her struggle with the eyelets completed, she carefully slides each shoe into a perfect line by the side of the bed.

Perched on the rushed kitchen seat, her toes ranged in a row down its rungs, The Child awaits the expected scolding. Cook, holding in one hand the rag with which she has mopped up the track of puddles, pulls out a chair, slowly smoothes its top rail and then sits down. Pained discernment fills her eyes. The Child's small hand slides slowly over the table toward a pile of large, freshly baked sugar cookies. Cook moves them away then arising from her seat deposits them one by one in the crock that stands on the counter by the flour bin. After a moment's reflection, she moves the full crock to the top shelf of the cupboard.

The Child, first forms the wet mop rag into a square then folds it again crosswise against itself.

Cook sighs deeply. "Your father, child, he not live the day. No more cookies."

On her steel bed cranked to its lowest setting the Old Woman turns back a crocheted counterpane of knotted yellow roses. The trembling tips of her fingers smooth the cover. Next she precisely folds the sheet to meet the spread's trellis of roses. She then lifts out from under the bolster a small pillow ticked in hard straw. With difficulty she climbs under the covers. She then sets the pillow at a slight elevation to aid her breathing during the night's long middle reaches.

The TV taps Fred Astaire. The camera pans his feet. Shiny black patent leather shoes flash. Faster and faster they whirl. The Old Woman does not see; her dimming eyes have squeezed closed. Blindly, she reaches for the drawer in the bedside table of antique, country pine. Her hand finds the open edge. Her fingers blunder but, at length, slowly, daintily, they pick up a cookie.

She eats with deliberate tiny bites. The convexed fingers delicately brush away each crumb.

The first cookie finished, she reaches for another and then for a third. Each is eaten slowly, with precise care, the crumbs swept.

"Thank you, Father," she says.

Her eyes open to the TV across the room. On its screen an athletic type, large glass of tea in hand, plunges backward into a deep pool. The tea does not spill. It refreshes. He drinks it.

The Old Woman's fingers achieve momentary cooperation. She reaches for the tumbler on her bedside stand.

"Mother, May I have a drink of cool water?" she asks.

Her voice, rising from an initial whisper, takes on strength, bounces off the white walls, rises to a shout above the announcer's babble.

As The Old Woman drinks slowly, deeply, the incessant light from the TV set glints off the tin picture frame on the dresser. A bit of light picks up the gold of the bowknot pinned to the dimity afternoon dress now discarded in a heap on the floor. The discarded glass tumbler glows empty, dry. The cookie crumbs remaining on the counterpane cast little shadows over its clusters of yellow roses. The Old Woman's head rests on the little round pillow ticked hard with straw. Her fingers relax beside her.

Finally, ninety years later, she smiles.

From between two rows of polished white teeth,
the announcer blows his audience a goodnight kiss.

CASTE IRON

Observations in Black and White

My partner and I, we're doing business in up-country Carolina. Folks here have their habits. Eating well is one of them.

We've feasted on this trip: fried chicken, cheese grits, scalloped tomatoes, hush puppies, and lemon meringue pie. Delectable. Sorry they don't develop the same *cachet* when prepared in my sleek northern kitchen. Never mind, we're here, into a new experience, beginning at table.

A week ago a bubbly little waitress half my age giggled as she taught me how to answer when she asked, "Sweet or unsweet?" At first I thought she meant the sauce for my catfish, but it's an iced tea question. And it's only a cultural opener; there's more to being born south of the Mason Dixon Line than making the choice between tea tasting like a second cousin to cold syrup and tea straight up with ice.

I shouldn't be telling you this story. Folks in these parts live by a different set of rules and I haven't had the experience necessary to comprehend more than a few of the contradictions. Take for example the proud white houses. Out front, acres of velvet lawn, requiring about four hours twice weekly sitting astride a riding mower, singing *Dixie*, making wide smooth arches round and round the thick trunks of massive magnolias.

On the other hand, out in back of these same white houses with their trimmed velvet lawns and blooming magnolias, things take a turn. Close enough to toss a ham bone across for the dogs to growl over, all that soft green lawn butts into a dismal tangle of forest. Venture one step out of the backyard sun, and thorns with daggers spiked for business meet you first thing. Like the straight razor Uncle Ted strops on his granddaddy's old strap each morning, these thorns bayonet painful reminders that they've been twisting around and between and underneath solid magnolia trunks for much longer than anyone breathing today can easily recall.

Across the front veranda it's a parade of formal columns, another world out back. Out front fine folks mount the broad verandah steps to a wide door opening onto a spacious reception hall. Fresh flowers grace an Empire table, and a gentle curve of stair draws the eye upward to the portrait of the great-grandmother who threatened to brain Sherman's officer with her shoe for the hatchet cuts his rogues dug into her prized hand-carved cherry banister.

Beyond the stairs the wide hall continues directly to the back door opening onto a service porch where black servants accomplish all the ordinary household chores. There are double locks on that back door. Heavy iron locks crafted by black slaves at white masters' orders for a bolted separation. Unmistakable markers for white front, black rear.

Strangely enough there are two sets of keys for this heavy iron lock. One dangles from a hook in the hall above the current master's narrow brimmed hat. The other hangs outside, from a peg above the antique washstand on the back porch. One set inside, the other outside. Either will open the door.

Back to iced tea. Sweet or unsweet? The first of the front/white, back/black basics for neophyte travelers such as myself.

My partner and I, we're two weeks into this southern excursion, so I reckon that I'm picking up on at least some of the rudiments. For example, at the fish house last night talking up one of our deals, we're seated opposite a table of four: middle aged couple, young couple. The older couple sits with their backs toward us. The daughter, whose face is a feminine version of her father's, looks right in my direction. Over the top of my menu I read her lips. She's telling her daddy that she's twenty and grown up enough to make her own decisions.

I think, "Classic. Daughter wants to do own thing. Daddy's not happy."

She flips one long blond strand back over her ear then leans forward talking earnestly.

Blond strand falls forward again.

She'd like to strike a bargain.

The young man seated next to her is not saying much. I can't see him too well because of the older woman's back, but I take him to be about eighteen at first, then remember how couples fresh out of teenhood almost always have the woman looking the more mature which means this young man is about twenty. Still, he's something more of a fledgling, fists clenched, determined to set up his own game.

The father has on a short sleeved plaid shirt. Blond hair sprouts from between sunspots farmed out along his forearms. There's a middle aged roll at his waist. That pudge comes from working cotton all day from a padded seat inside an air conditioned cab after a breakfast of pink smoked ham, yellow eyes on the eggs, red-eye gravy on the grits, butter on the biscuits and a quarter cup of cream topping the coffee. He forks at a plate of deep fried flounder with stubby fingers arranged across his palm like the unbending rows in his cotton fields.

No sound from the mother who's dressed in dark green polyester. An inverted box pleat down the back of her homemade flowered shirt allows more give in the region of an ample front. Her permed hair twists to non-descript collar-length. From where I sit there's no face to her, nor any hint of a lineage ready to trade an officer's brains for the destruction of a cherry banister either. The family's pride has nested in the daughter, whose own face would be a good oval if it weren't for the square line of her jaw.

Our tables share a waiter who refills the daughter's iced-tea glass from the same pitcher he's used for mine. For her he adds extra ice. She freeze-eyes him with a practiced, "Screw-you," turns back to her father.

I gather the daughter and the waiter know each other. Schoolmates?

Between bites of slaw, I continue my surreptitious lip-reading. Daughter is very definitely certain she will finish the university.

Up to this point father has said nothing that negotiates the space between our tables. But now he's turned his head a bit, so I catch the tense line of his mouth, down hard at its edges, twitching as he stares at the outsized fisherman's trap netted into restaurant decor above our heads.

An order of lobster and crab legs arrives at our table balanced on the left shoulder of the waiter. This young man wears two little gold earrings, walks with a smooth from-the-hip swing, and serves hot ceramic platters as if plates double easily for the ball he knows how to spin smartly into the hands of a waiting receiver.

I surmise, "Black man making it through higher education on a B-ball scholarship and waiting tables for evening meals with tips."

We begin cracking open red legs and fins and pieces I think are backs, but maybe they're thick necks. I'm not up on crustacean anatomy, and in this setting asking too many questions bumps me into the poor-little-thing-from-up-north category.

The shell crackers are big and heavy like the ones we used for walnuts on my childhood's Pennsylvania farm. I know how to split nuts with them and how to let the nutmeat out whole, but snapping through red shells so I can pick at white meat is something new to me, slow going. Comes out in shreds and bitty pieces.

I've clamped onto a mouthful when the father at the next table finally says something short, sharp and punctuated with a push of his fish to the side of his plate. There's a quick glance between daughter and boyfriend. It's a good bet they're holding hands under the table because she's awkward with the fork in her left.

No crying or anything, but there's an intense connection between her eyes and what's she's pushing around with that left-handed fork.

I want more from her boyfriend's face, but it wears one of those mulatto masks. There's not a wrinkle beneath the dark curls that bounce in a neat line above his ears. His eyes are dark too, big, and expressionless, except when he takes a guarded sideways glance at his girl.

Very, very cautious, those sideways glances.

Wariness bred on the black side of an old plantation's cast iron locks?

The waiter, he's donned a darker mask that closes in even tighter when I ask him about himself. I like to check out my first-impression guesses about waiters. Are they working nights to keep themselves in school, or supporting a habit like stock car racing, or both?

The night before last in another restaurant, the waitress treated us to her complete life history starting with the fact that she's not prejudiced, ending with how she'd cut her sister off cold if the, '*bitch* didn't drop her *nigger* boyfriend.' In-between expletives, this Twiggy-blond high school senior, planning on college and responsibly sleeping with her long-term boyfriend, managed to let us know how much she loves children and how she wants to work professionally in early childhood education teaching dear little Tommy Roberts and Bonnie Jeans.

That was the night before last.

Tonight, Waiter-of-the-Gold-Earrings tells me he's a student, no details, no smile and eyes focused on an invisible spot above my head.

But I catch him making eye contact with the boyfriend at the next table. A covert visual message that shouts, "Cut this white girlfriend business now," slipped in with more-than-needed extras on ice for a basketball buddy's tea.

Boyfriend dumps in two packet's worth of sweetener. Uses a fierce full hand press to wad the paper. Gives it a right hand flip to the floor in the waiter's direction.

My table passes biscuits. Scrumptious wickedness, but this is Carolina up-country and we're eating out, so we send Mr. Gold Earrings for more.

Time-out at the next table. The father's eyes still fix on the lobster trap above his head. Maybe he can't figure his way out, like that big squirrel we caught recently in the animal control's heavy wire box. Creature tried every move. Even broke a tooth gnawing at the metal bars.

The daughter is forking, with her right hand now. Boyfriend's picking his way one by one through a pile of mouth sized scallops, chewing with care lest they lodge in the throat. The mother endures, still unreadable.

At my table we're nervously activating bottom line deals. Except for me, we're mostly ignoring the neighbors. At a stalemate in deal-making our conversation wings into bemoaning the post-X generations.

"Post everything, that's the current crop," my dinner companions tell me. "The one just coming up into twenty. They've got their ideas about mixing things up."

I'm minding my own plate, licking butter and honey off my fingers, half monitoring the flow of my table's talk as it wallows ever deeper into an aging boomer version of the regional basics.

"And now the government's behind this mixed-up stuff which is sad because these days people pay no mind to the way things ought to be done."

"Those in government today don't know how to set the proper boundaries. Coddle the blacks. Forget morals; they've gone out with TV."

"No account to mix things up, if you know what I mean. Spells trouble."

By this time we've downed three refills on dry burgundy; so the pitch has climbed higher. The neighbor table can surely hear.

However, all's very quiet. The father gets up. With one firm gesture he places his narrow brimmed hat on the precise center top of his head. He then helps his wife to her feet.

She hunches over her purse, clutches it close.

The girl gets up too, in a kind of a jump.

The boyfriend unwinds from his seat as if he's rising from the bench to enter the game.

The girl is a mixture: determined in the line of her jaw, nervous in the twist of her fingers.

Father picks up the check. Mother takes a single step, stumbles. Father propels her by the elbow toward the lobby door. They exit.

Momentarily, this couple done in black and white stands there. He has her hand. Lightly, then tight. There's a long look between them. Blue mascara digs a slow wet ditch down her face. He'd like to cry too, but not in public, so they speed through the side door.

At our table we've reduced the mound on our plates by only half. The waiter brings doggie bags, takes my credit card.

"Know that couple?" I ask.

"Yeah," he says.

His eyes do an instant flicker, then shade down to an even darker disguise.

My tablemates, who've taken in the tears and the side door exit, shrug.

"You're a Yankee," they tell me, "don't try to understand the South."

And I'm thinking tea. Sweet. Unsweet. Both with ice, more or less. The truth is I can't stomach frigid syrup that hides basic flavors. Something hot and black would taste mighty fine after this dinner's stuffing. Besides that I've just recently developed a major sensitivity about locks on the insides of back doors, especially when it's clear there's been nothing to stop whole generations of white men from sneaking round to make forceful whoopee on the black side of those fine white houses.

My indignation quota climbs from high to highest. The waiter returns my credit card.

"That couple there, too bad," I tell him.

"Yeah," he says. "He's got no business messing with one of their kind."

There's more of the flash in his dark eyes and a grim line to his mouth; then that mask pulls itself down, neatly blocking my self-righteous pass at communication.

Like I say, I'm a Yankee, off when it comes to knowing what's in the mix down here. Apparently, those old iron locks work from both the White and the Black sides of the door.

COUNTRY AUCTION

A cut glass bowl and six silver teaspoons

If you folks just drive up to the top of this little hill you'll find lots of parking by the side of the road. Plenty of shade near the big maple behind that white house. While you get parked, I'll get you a card with a number so you can get your bids in. Nice stuff here today. Good crowd too, some local and some not. We've just gotten going so you've not missed much.

Benson, you say your name is; Rogers mine. Been helping the ladies out with their auction for some years now. Know the history of this local stuff, and how to sniff out what's behind a bargain too. Quite sharp at it, if I say so myself, when I put my mind to it that is.

The beds, dressers and such are over here. Under those walnuts there's tables of smaller things: glass, kitchenware and so on. Church ladies set up this auction as a fundraiser. This year they're counting on a good percentage, enough to buy new pew cushions. There's Sadie over there seated by the tables on that folding chair, the bleached blond lady, fanning herself. She's had a deal of cleaning out to do lately. Just sold her mother's house. Looks to cash in on the accumulation she's had to haul out. Not bad stuff some of it. Has a history too. That's down my alley. Take the butter churn there. I 'spect Sadie found that piece in the basement. We had one just like that when I was a kid. Milked the cow every morning and evening. That was my job. Took a full pail into my mother. She let the milk set a day to rise and then skimmed off the top. Poured that cream into a gallon jar like the one over there and turned the crank. Weren't much work, and did get us right sweet butter.

See those glass canning jars in that basket there? Not a nick in one of them. They remind me of when my mother and sisters used to slave over the kettles in the July heat when the peaches come in.

For peaches, to get to the flesh you have to slide the skins off when they're hot and slippery and hard to hang on to. After that you fight to hold on to them while you cut out the stone, then fight them again as you pack the jars. Juice will run sweet and sticky down your fingers. Good licking, but it will slick the floor. Like as not some younguns will be running about the kitchen pulling at skirts wanting this and that. In this life there's always something hard to hold on to or getting in the way of what needs to be done.

As I say, Sadie will get about eighty dollars for the churn and the canning jars.

Sadie's new at having her mother to worry about like she does now. It frets her considerable to have the hindrance. Martha always took care of their folks, let Sadie live her own life. Imagine Sadie feels the need to get away. I expect she'll huff herself off on the bus to visit grandkids when this is all over.

There were two of them, Sadie, the first, and Martha, the baby. On that next table Sadie's got her sister's set of blue glass dishes. Martha collected them from soap powder boxes. Rather unusual to see a complete set. Most people lack the patience to put the whole thing together piece by piece. Martha never did use the dishes much. Kept them for show in the parlor china cabinet. I remember a time ago when I worked at the mercantile. You passed it there at the crossroads on the northeast corner. Martha would come in to look over all them soap boxes just to see what piece of blue glass she wanted to get next. The stuff has a right pretty color when the light shines through it. Sadie's got Martha's whole set there, plates and glasses and those little bowls. The auctioneer will target the ladies for them. You can bet somebody pays a fair price just to put them on show the way Martha did.

You know, there's a sad tale there. Martha got herself killed a couple of months back in a car accident. Seems some kid had been down to Sedalia and nipped a bit too much. Went through a stop sign right into Martha. Sheriff's got him working on the roads over by Blackburn. Locks him up at night. Figures a bit of this heat will burn the liquor out of him if nothing else will. To my mind it might do more to raise his thirst. Nobody knows just what Martha was doing at one in the morning going north by Sweet Springs. Sadie says Martha had been to a collector's show in Kansas City and probably decided to come back to Elmwood rather than spend the night. Appears logical. I don't do much with gossip, especially when them that's in it is gone to their reward.

Look here. Did you see this, a real old timey Victrola with the white dog on it and all. Must have hauled it down from the attic at Mrs. Trent's. That's Alma, Sadie and Martha's mother. I haven't seen an old Victrola like this in some time now. Records too, a bunch of them. We used to gather on Mr. And Mrs. Peters' porch of an evening and set there to listen to theirs. One of us had to sit inside to keep the old thing cranked. Peters had a record by an Irish man, Harry Lauder I think his name was, who could sing and sing. He would get out those old empire songs like the *Road to Mandalay* so you could just see that gold sun coming up out of the bay like glory itself.

Tommy Peters went to school with Martha and me. Served over there in those oriental parts, the time of the Second World War with the *Japs* and all. Long before 'Nam. Tommy got himself captured by the *Japs* and put into one of those camps like you can see in the Kwai bridge movie. Not a pretty thing that, but Tommy he was built stout as a good rail. Made it through, he did. Kept almost all of him, minus just his feet and a bit of trouble with a knee. He's got some artificial things from the government. Does right well with them. Can't farm much, though. When his Old Man, Jake Peters, passed, Tommy got the farm with their Victrola, the porch and all, lived there with his mother and drove into the government office in Sedalia for work. In fact, still lives there. That place of his is about two mile down the road from where the McPherson kid ran into Martha two months ago.

City folks like you come out here looking for good things cheap, but nowadays most of the dealers have raked through the place long since. The local folks know that all they have to do with a really good piece the kids don't want is pick up the phone. Till the accident, Martha acted as a dealer's representative. She let Kansas City people know what was stashed in every attic around here. Every parlor too. Folks didn't mind trading through her, she being a local and all. And she was fair. Martha must have made some money from it, enough to pay on that new Buick she was driving the night of the accident.

Martha had a habit of putting aside some of the lesser things she come across to sell on her own. Today Sadie's offering those things Martha had collected just waiting for the ladies' sale. They're on this next table and Sadie says they will go one hundred percent to the pew cushions.

This bowl, real cut glass, and the half dozen silver teaspoons sure are fine. Pride myself on the history of everything in this neighborhood. Martha must of got these from Tommy Peters. But he's not been letting go of his mother's stuff. Sadie says she doesn't know except that they were in the car the night of the accident, on the front seat too. Can't picture the bowl not being broken in the crash. Car's windows were. In these parts silver spoons and such are most likely to pass to the grandkids. Can't think that anyone's done different in some time. Can't picture Tommy giving them up either.

Folks said Martha should have married Tommy Peters, but then she never did. I remember eating

Sunday dinner at the Peters any number of times when we was growing up. My but Mrs. Peters did set a swell table. The ladies always talked about it. Used her silver, she did, and lots of cut glass. Inherited the glass from her family somehow, an aunt they say. She had this bowl set out on the buffet so as it would catch the light. Sun would shine through pretty of an afternoon. Folks said Mrs. Peters had so much cut glass that she'd gone to storing it wrapped in worn blankets under the beds.

Well now folks don't let my jawing keep you from browsing about. Auctioneer will get through with that big stuff in a moment now and then he'll move directly to these tables.

Bid on that cut glass bowl did you? *One hundred dollars even!* A right good price. As you say, make a nice wedding gift for your granddaughter. Settle yourselves here in the shade of the church for a time to cool off a bit. Yes, I bet you haven't seen anybody whittling in some time. My granddad took me to his knee and showed me how when I was just a little thing. Whittling sets me to thinking about our mystery here, about how Martha got Mrs. Peters' bowl and those silver spoons. I've been thinking Tommy could have given them to her to sell. Can't right blame him not wanting to keep them up, but still that's not like him.

Tommy was close to his mother. Kept things just

like she left them since her passing. That's about a year now. He buried her out in the old family plot along with all the Peters. Their plot's in a grove of those original oaks just over by the road before you turn into their place. Been located there since Tommy's great, great granddad homesteaded. Tommy keeps it up real nice. He had George Wentz put up a fancy iron fence where the old rock wall fell apart on the north side. I would have heard if Tommy had let go of his mother's cut glass or silver spoons.

Maybe he gave them to Martha, you say. Now there's a thought. Tommy gave Martha the cut glass bowl and the silver spoons. That makes some sense don't it. He was sweet on her in high school, but she paid him no mind, went out with Joe Guenther, if my memory serves me right. After graduation, Tommy and Joe went off to the army. I did my turn in the navy. Didn't see much action though. Joe didn't come back. His folks went to see his grave in France somewhere.

Martha didn't leave town. She worked at the mercantile. After Tommy come back, folks thought they might get together, but somehow they never did. Martha didn't pay him much mind and Tommy stuck to his government job in town and to his home on the farm. He wasn't strange, just quiet, with his feet like they were and all. Even when we was growing up, never did have much to say. The ladies claim his mother took up all his time, but that's just gossip and I don't get into those things. Myself, I've always been over there rather regular, especially of a summer evening to set out on the porch and talk about the weather or the state of the roads. Tommy had himself a new Dodge all fixed up so he could drive it and his mother kept a nice house. When we'd set out on that porch of an evening she always served cool mint tea with silver soda straws that had hearts for spoons at their bottoms. Then Mrs. Peters passed quietly one night. Tommy found her in her bed the next morning.

Come to think of it, I was in the house for Mrs. Peters' viewing and that bowl you just bought was sitting on the buffet exactly where it always had been. That was about a year ago. Tommy's gone on living there by himself, has Anna Wentz in to clean. Does his own cooking. Nowadays there's no mint tea on the porch. Tommy serves beer, Miller Lite. Anna says that he gave her a key. Said he wanted things left as they were. That's all Anna says.

What was Martha doing all this time, you say? Well, she lived with her folks in that white house you parked behind. Convenient to the mercantile and she had her flower garden. Her folks needed care, especially of late with Alma so bound up arthritic and Jed feeble and stone deaf. Got so some nights you could hear his TV all the way over to where we're sitting now. Jed died just about the same time as Mrs. Peters, about a week apart.

Sadie's been living over in Blackburn for years. She and Ed married young. Had five kids. So naturally the care of the folks fell to Martha even after Ed, that's Sadie's husband, passed a while back. Neighbors said those girls had some words after Ed's funeral, but the only change was that Sadie came over to sit when Martha had to go to Kansas City and might not get back till late. Sadie put her mother in that nursing home quick as a whistle after she had charge. Alma wasn't too happy, but Sadie says she'll adjust. The house's been sold to help pay for her care. The new school principal bought it day after it went on the market. Good for his family. There's three kids of his and one of his wife's.

Martha got into the antique business after the mercantile cut back. She needed the money. Always was one to care for beautiful things. Her roses were something to look at like that pink one on the fence. She planted it quite a while ago. Real beauty in June. Undertaker laid her out with a bouquet of those pink roses in her hands. Before the accident Martha worked at the mercantile a couple of days a week, then she'd spend the rest visiting folks and transporting things into Kansas City to the dealers. Took to staying in town more often. The drive's not that long, but business kept her.

Haven't seen Tommy here today. Not easy for him to get about with the roll in this lawn and all. Doesn't come to town much anymore. Shopped at the mercantile till about a month ago, but the steps got to him even though the kids that work there tote his sacks and help him about. In fact, I've been busy, haven't seen him much at all lately. Tommy just sat in his car at Martha's funeral.

When you think of it, what's a fellow like Tommy going to do to get a girl's attention, especially when she's paid him no mind for years on end? Well, in his quiet way he just might try appealing to her sense of business. He might try to hook her with some proposition about a cut glass bowl and silver spoons. Ask her to get an estimate on value or something like that. Maybe she stopped by that last evening to have a look at Mrs. Peters' things and they got to discussing, on the porch. It got late, with Sadie sitting Alma and all. Finally she drove off with the bowl and the spoons and a promise to get back in touch. Down the road just two miles she met her end. Maybe she was driving, thinking about something new, while that boy who hit her wasn't thinking at all. There it is folks.

Think I'll tell the auctioneer I'll top any bid he gets on those spoons. Return them to Tommy tonight. They'll help me tell him I understand how he's been feeling so down lately. No, keep the bowl. I'll tell Tommy you bought it for a wedding gift for your granddaughter. He'll find that a comfort.

ELEVATOR

A family of many quirks

It's the week before Christmas. Mrs. Grass is stuck in the elevator. That's between fifth and sixth. No, she is not hurt, just stuck and wants to get out. She has been out, at the grocery, purchasing the ingredients for her Christmas cookies. She is not yelling yet, just talking to herself and pounding on the door. Pushing the buttons too, as if that would do any good. Mildred, down on first, shouts to her through the metal grill. "Keep calm," she bellows.

Terry, the new manager, has gone up the stairs to see what he can do. He mutters that she's probably pushed all the buttons so the damn thing's got stuck on neutral. If Terry can't get there faster, Mrs. Grass will start screaming and then somebody will call the fire department for their emergency crew. It would be interesting to see her coming up to sixth hanging on to a rope. Emerging with that overloaded green plastic string bag of hers clenched tightly on top of her multiple mid-drift. But then she couldn't hold on. Somebody would have to climb through the trap and lift her out, groceries and all.

The elevator has not been working at all right lately. Two days ago Elvira, who routinely pushes all the buttons, got stuck and yelled down the shaft that they're not to tell her to shut up. Just get her out so she can get to her ladies' circle. They are set to decorate the church tree and she wants it done in blue.

John on eighth keeps a dog, a brown mutt of limited distinction, but quiet manners in his two-by-four studio. John is seventy, he says, and maybe that figures out about right if you allow for ten laid aside somewhere. The dog and John use the stairs going down for exercise and then take the elevator back up. The dog looks like an animal who has never met four legged spunk, and maybe not two legged either. Outside their apartment John short leashes his beast into a nose-at-heel stroll. Even in December's cold they duo in the morning down the street south and in the afternoon across the street north, or on Troost Avenue where John claims he's told the loafers hanging about the bar that he'll sic his dog on them. "That's why those bums don't bother me," John says. John's always coming up on the elevator, the dog always in tow. John says he's been in and out of this building for sixty years...celebrated the holidays here for twenty five. Place used to be swell he remembers, bell hops and all that. "There's not anybody who's been about here who doesn't know me," he says. John tells Terry, the new manager, he'll be pleased to help Mrs. Grass find the right button next time.

Standing, hands on hips, by the lobby elevator door Elvira harrumphs at John's talk. Says she's been in the neighborhood since she was born and moved into the building twenty-seven years ago and will be here when they carry him and his mousy dog out to the pound. "Neighborhood's gone down a lot since the second war," she says. "Used to be a lovely restaurant on the corner...served flaming rum cake at Christmas and lots of fancy things. Look at what's there now," she says. "Can't even get to the grocery store for my decors without passing some guy taking a piss by the curb."

Terry has two boys who skateboard. Wild flying loops in the parking lot when their father's eye turns elsewhere which it mostly is. There is a sign up saying Terry will get the elevator fixed. Elvira, who has gotten stuck twice already this week, says she's talked to him, but it's plain that he's more worried about Ruth whose blue eyes twinkle when Pavarotti sings *Ave Maria* on TV. Ruth puts up little signs inviting everyone to come watch with her...bring your own popcorn and cokes. Those cranky metal doors might crush Ruth who cannot bark like Elvira nor move as fast either. Ruth is to call Terry when she wants to come downstairs so he can come get her.

Puss is a cat, a real one, three legs, who lives on sixth. Puss rides contentedly, independently, up and down, up and down...always in the same corner observing everything, giving everyone her long inscrutable glare which says don't you dare rat on me. No one does. Puss gives John's dog a friendly lick when he appears. They sit side by side.

This elevator is, you understand, located in a ten story apartment building in downtown Kansas City, Missouri. The time is the present that is to say the last decade of the twentieth century. Half the folks who live here are on social assistance. The other half of us live here because we like high ceilings and hand carved moldings even when the paint is peeling. The elevator's heavy doors don't pose a threat to us; for, when this cranky lift deep funks, jogs up and down the stairs are good for our health.

Susie's a snappy young lady, fresh from a western Kansas farm town, who does have a most interesting figure and who is quite new to the building and is, no doubt, in need of company. She does her laundry in the basement machines. Getting there means a ride up and down ten stories four times: one down to put her laundry in, one return up, down for the next load and so on. This is December, but she travels in one of those recently mod bathing outfits cut up to the waist on the sides and down to her navel in front. I know she is wondering why she's not getting much response. Trouble is the young fellows around here are mostly gay. She is frustrated. They are polite. Wonder how long it will take this cow-eyed *ingénue* (the girl who told me over the basement dryers last week that she'd left a starched white voile cap in the top drawer of a country dresser) to figure that one out?

Strange how people stop holding hands when I get into this thing. Must be my graying hair or maybe the academic air I fail to leave in the classroom. Yesterday, said as much to Joe and Pete, the two young men from the large end unit on ninth. They looked a bit sheepish at first, but then grinned in unison. Note under my door this morning: *Come to our place for drinks this afternoon at five*. Right on! These two watch TV with Rose, do her grocery shopping and take her to the concerts in the big city park on summer evenings. She calls them her sweet boys and bakes them cookies, since Thanksgiving, sugar Rudolphs with cinnamon dot noses.

Mildred lives on first. It is a good thing. When Mildred gets in, the elevator sighs to one foot below floor level. She doesn't use it much, just to go to the basement to do her laundry. She also keeps her Christmas cactus in the basement, in the dark for two months. That cactus is huge, diameter maybe five feet. Takes Terry, and Pete and Joe to maneuver the thing. Before Thanksgiving, the three of them hoist it up onto a cart while Mildred supervises. They deposit it in the lobby. To the left where the sun warms it most of the day. "It'll bloom for Christmas," Mildred proclaims. She stations herself by it each morning for her ten o'clock coffee plus two Danish. Pete, in from his all night gig, joins her sometimes, brings his own Danish.

At Christmas there's always a party for the residents. Decorating begins right after Thanksgiving. This year, Joe and Pete work on the lights until late one night. Joe's sense of order has them a steady, celestial white. The very next day after the two of them complete their late night, steady white light decorating stint, Mrs. Grass and Elvira and Mildred busy themselves with those same lights. By noon they have them blinking yellow and pink. Late in the day Mildred stations herself between the tree and her blooming cactus. Exactly at four thirty Joe arrives, ventures one look at the carnival, bows to Mildred and disappears into the elevator. "Poor lady, even John's mutt will not eat her cookies," he says to me going up. Puss, in her usual corner, yawns.

Susie, that's the girl in the December bathing suit, has taken to trailing Pete to the roof, sitting there yoga fashion while he practices. Pete has asked me to help him reroute her. I post a notice for the church young adults group, but she says she's left them behind in Kansas. We take her to a bar for country and western dancing. There's a young dance instructor. Susie needs lessons. Yesterday, the day before Christmas, I got on the elevator on fourth. There they stood, dance instructor and his rapt pupil, holding hands. They waved when I exited on seventh. That ponderous metal door lurched shut on a giggle.

Mildred has nickeled and dimed one dollar from each of us for the Christmas pot. One dollar doesn't go far unless it's added to a thousand of imagination. Pete chauffeurs Mildred to the Good Will where, she says, a dollar stretches like well chewed gum. This unlikely pair of elves find a romantic novel for Elvira, fancy pencils for the skateboarders. Mildred sends Pete off for a can of tuna for three legged puss just so he wouldn't know about the *Sweet Adeline* sheet music the girl at the cash register hides for his surprise. Together Mildred and Pete dig a green sweater out of the fifty-percent-off-baby-ware bin for John's mutt. In the end they have a big box of cinnamon for Joe, pliers for Terry, a black lace camisole for Susie, a blue wool scarf for John. Pete, with a wink to the cash register girl, slides plant food for Mildred into his pocket. There's a new belt buckle for Santa and a zebra pin for me. I know about the pin early because I help Mildred wrap. We recycle the paper from last year. The skateboarders donate ribbon, recently lifted from Walgreen's down the block.

Yesterday morning as Santa descended to check on preparations for the residents' party, he got stuck between fifth and sixth. In real life Santa is Mr. Sweeny from the end unit on eighth. He has been Santa for a number of years now. Mildred says it's ten, but John says it's more than that. Mr. Sweeny doesn't need to use pillows to fill out the uniform and he practices...does the part in the mall on Mondays and Wednesdays during the season. Yesterday Terry prepared to winch him out with a rope. Pete climbed down onto the top of the elevator cage and opened the trap door. He got inside with Mr. Sweeny.

They improvised a rope swing. Santa Sweeny sat in it. They hoisted. But this Father Christmas proved bigger than the opening. His bulky costume could easily tear. Pete helped him disrobe. Terry and Joe loosened the bolts on the metal panels to widen the hole. Pete pushed. Terry and Joe pulled. They got him out, shook out his costume, buttoned him back into it. Puffing mightily Santa left for his job in the mall.

And now Mrs. Grass is stuck. Terry comes with the rope, but has only to push the right combination of buttons. The elevator lurches downward. Comes to a stop at the lobby. Terry helps her up the stairs to tenth then runs back down for the green plastic bag of groceries.

A week later it's Christmas. Santa Sweeny arrives at the party via the back stairs, showers all with candies and opens his pack. Puss is there on the front row. John's dog sits beside her. The skate boarders skid into places beside them. Elvira gives the boys a shove with her good foot. The younger flashes her the finger. His brother calls him a dope, thumps him on the head. Santa hands out the gifts. Mrs. Grass recycles the paper and the ribbon.

Ruth has knitted red and blue mittens for everyone. She has worked on them since August. (Joe purchased the yarn.) The mittens hang on the tree where yellow and pink intermittently purple them royal. Each is tagged with a name inscribed precisely in Ruth's tiny script. Mildred checks the names. The skateboarders hand them out.

Mrs. Grass's best lace cloth graces the table. Elvira has saved the paper tea napkins with gold angels since last January's sale. There is ginger ale in pink punch to go with mounds of frosted cookies. Terry shelters a bottle of some harder stuff on the floor behind his seat. Joe has baked a dark fruitcake topped by a rich sugar sauce. Susie and her dancing friend stumble downstairs, sleepy eyed, just in time for the last two pieces. Santa presents that black lace camisole then ogle eyes as she snugs it down over her bright red T-neck. Mrs. Grass and Elvira compliment Mildred on her cactus. "It's glory all over with those red blossoms," they tell her. The blossoms turn purple, again. Mildred shares cookies with John and with tiny Ruth who peeks out from the depths of the plushy sofa pillows. Ruth hums as Pete slides his horn through variations on *Away in the Manger*. Terry's kids leave to try their new skateboards.

The elevator, remarkably, is working. Joe escorts Ruth back up to her apartment. Elvira, clutching four cookies, her new mittens, and the new novel ascends with them. John says he'll just sit by the tree for a while. "My heart," he says to me. Santa Sweeney joins him. "We've got Christmas, family style," he says.

Puss, curled up under the tree, opens one eye. Her nose twitches at her tuna on a pink paper plate an inch from the end of her whiskers. Pete turns to clean up the dishes. Mildred supervises. Mrs. Grass lends a hand. I take John's dog, all done up in his new green sweater, out for a turn around the block.

Baby for Dinner

Sister loved her little pig
Its eyes were china blue
And everywhere that Sister went...

Baby cried all night. Eating her proved to be the best solution.

It started round about ten on a bright spring morning when Hofsteader's sow delivered herself of a dozen sturdy piglets plus one pathetic runt. Sister had wandered down the road to watch. Mother welcomed the birthing as an opportunity for practical education now that Sister had reached eight and couldn't be put off when she asked questions such as, "Why do daddy goats climb on top of mommy goats?"

Eyes squeezed shut, the runt could hardly bring herself into balance on four spindly legs let alone attempt to quiver her way over the pile of her eager siblings as they pushed themselves into dinner from their mama's great broadside.

"That one's not likely to make it," Hofsteader mumbled. Scooping up the runt in his big red hand he presented it to Sister who carried it back up the road to Mother's kitchen in the front pocket of her green pinafore.

There by the warm coils of the steam radiator Sister set up her baby in an apple box lined with old linen dish towels and last year's rosy flannel nightshirt. After consuming a tummy-full of formula improvised of warm skim milk and sugar syrup, served from a doll-sized plastic bottle, Baby poked her tiny pink snout into a fold of the rosy flannel nightshirt and slept. All the remainder of the daylight hours that is.

When the supper dishes had been washed, dried and put back in the cupboards, and the full black of the night had swallowed even the boldest of shadows, Baby stretched her little legs, blinked her tiny eyes and broke into sobs. Her plaintive squeals skidded underneath the kitchen door, bounced up the back stairs, and with growing vigor invaded the back bedroom where they shook Sister awake.

Aroused from her own sleep, Mother helped Sister assemble the midnight bottle. Kneeling on the hard cracks of the linoleum floor, Sister fed her new charge. Finally satiated Baby rolled onto her side, her tiny eyes squeezed tightly shut. Sister tucked her back into the apple box for the night. Mother flipped off the light switch.

An instant later, Baby moaned.

"Leave her," Mother commanded.

Sucking on the hem of her pajama top, Sister followed Mother up the back stairs to her little room above the kitchen. There she slowly slid beneath her quilt of pieced gingham on which Mary ran down the hill while her cotton ball lamb gamboled at her heels.

No sooner had she settled herself than Baby's cries mounted into a shrieked crescendo. This time Sister crept alone down the back stairs to the rescue. So it happened that Baby spent the remainder of that night, the next, and the next curled in a contented ball in the crook of Sister's arm. Smiling in her sleep, Sister pulled the gingham quilt over both their heads.

Naturally, Baby grew. By mid-June, her pointy ears sticking out through the slits Sister had sliced in a frilly doll cap, she toddled along behind as they strolled down the lane to the creek where they shared peanut butter sandwiches and celery sticks in the shade of an old willow. Later both of them munched on the daisies. As a result Sister gave her pet a new name, Daisy. "Because," she told anyone who took the trouble to ask, "because she's lovely and warm like the sun in the center."

By mid-July an ever more corpulent Baby Daisy ran about on four sturdy legs. Her diet consisted of warm milk, sugar syrup, peanut butter sandwiches and flowers. Daisy didn't discriminate when it came to flowers. Mother's manicured geraniums, petunias, and summer lilies tasted just fine.

And so it happened that one steamily hot afternoon when Mother braked her shiny black Chrysler to a stop in the drive, Daisy waddled over in greeting. The last of Mother's prize royal purple petunias trailed from the corner of her mouth. Mother looked the happy pig straight in her blue eyes and said in a most carefully controlled voice, "This is the end, young lady." From the car's trunk Mother took a shiny metal stake, a long chain, and a metal studded dog collar.

At first Daisy, accustomed to fancy touches, liked the collar. Besides she soon learned that when she wanted to wander, an appropriate shake of her head would send it sliding off the end of her long nose. Sister moved her doll housekeeping to an empty corn crib within easy reach of Daisy's chain and managed to provide an extra ration of exquisite treats: chocolates snitched from the sideboard in the dining room, ice-cream bars slipped from the freezer, fancy carrot sticks from the tray prepared for Mother's luncheon guests.

Sister and Daisy still slept under the quilt in the small upstairs room. Daisy wore diapers, but there were the inevitable, unfortunate accidents. After one unusually messy slop of blackberry mixed with the tender tops of the vegetable garden's beets, Mother directed the hired boy to complete a secure pen in a corner of the goat shed. Here Daisy would sleep in the company of the dozen resident goats.

On the appointed day, Sister spread an entire bale of straw on the floor of Daisy's new bed while her unsuspecting pet happily nosed into the small nest of a terrified field mouse. Under Mother's stern gaze, Sister placed an especially full dish of warm mash mixed with meat scraps and brown gravy next to the automatic water fountain by the door of Daisy's stall.

That night Sister sat at the top of the back stairs and wept into the wee hours. Standing guard, Mother forbade any step further. First Daisy bawled and then she bellowed. Relenting, Mother pulled a green robe over her flannel nightgown. Her slippers flopping she made her way to the shed where she tried in vain to persuade the largest nanny goat to bed down with the inconsolable Daisy. Finally, forced into frustrated retreat, Mother left in such confusion that she neglected to secure the gate to the pen. The next morning the hired boy found the entire herd of goats in the orchard nibbling green apples. Daisy, who had expanded her idea of family, happily munched right along with them.

When school began again that fall the hired boy and Sister climbed onto the school bus before seven each morning. The boy, whose duties required that he rise before the sun to complete the milking, then turned the goats into their pasture. Daisy, whose record by now sentenced her to solitary confinement unless accompanied by an able bodied human, remained in her pen. Sister saw to her fresh water and ample provisions. Daisy, now somewhat more composed with age, ate and slept and grew fat.

One day the bull snake who lived in the remnants of the barn walls wandered too far from his accustomed routes right through the crack in the goat shed door. Perhaps he was hunting the mouse that lived exceptionally well on the cracked corn left over from Daisy's abundance. Daisy, thoroughly bored with snatching at the flies that circled her nose, joined in the hunt. In one purposeful lunge she splintered the bottom boards of her pen. The snake barely escaped her sharp hooves as a joyfully liberated Daisy made her way through the open barnyard gate to the kitchen door. There she banged and bellowed for her accustomed admittance.

With her mouth drawn into a hard line, Mother called Mr. Hofsteader. Sensing an emergency, he dispatched his truck at once with two hired hands wise in the ways of animals. Daisy eagerly accepted the first apple they offered, but when a second offering rolled against the truck's back tires she sniffed danger. Wary of Daisy's considerable bulk and the razor qualities of her sharp teeth, the men approached with caution. All four feet cutting firmly through the straw covering Mother's priceless Dutch bulbs, Daisy held her ground.

"That's a smart one," the men told Mother, "but don't you worry, Misses, we'll nab her."

A stout rope spun about their heads and lassoed Daisy about her mid-section. Screaming her indignation, Daisy found herself pushed and tugged up the truck ramp then shoved into a far corner where she bit furiously at the links chaining her to the back of the cab.

"That's an ornery one, Misses," the men said, "but we've got her for you."

Grateful, Mother offered black coffee and slices of deep-dish apple pie.

Completely unaware of Daisy's struggle for survival, Sister completed her school sums perfectly. Her skilled reading aloud to the class earned her a promotion from the Bluebirds to the Robins. For Show-and-Tell she pulled out the chart she had made of Daisy's weight gain from the day the runt had ridden home in her pinafore pocket.

"We love each other," she told the class.

Nobody laughed.

By one of the Lord's mercies Sister didn't see the butchering, which kept Mr. Hofsteader's knives busy for all of an hour and a half. By the end of the day what was left of Daisy lay on the farmer's kitchen table wrapped in white paper packages neatly labeled chops, tenderloin, and ribs. In the meantime Mrs. Hofsteader bustled about boiling scraps with handfuls of seasonings then poured them into molds to set for scrapple. Since she knew Mother would not want them, she tucked the cleaned pig's feet into a corner of her own freezer. Lastly she began to process the brain for headcheese. The next evening Mr. Hofsteader himself placed the white paper packages in Mother's basement freezer.

Sister, who'd said not a word when Mother told her what had happened to Daisy, watched from a crack in the kitchen door. She kept strangely quiet until after supper when Mother assigned the Saturday chores.

"No!" Sister put down her spoon very deliberately. "No," she repeated, hands in her lap and staring at the ceiling, "I will not clean out Daisy's pen."

Only slightly dismayed, Mother shook her head. "Never mind," she said. "The boy will take care of it when he tends to the goats."

Dinnertime Sunday Mother served roast pork loin along with white rice, thick pan gravy, the last of the summer squash, and applesauce with ginger cookies for dessert. Sister ate nothing except two exceptionally large slices of the roast.

Mother noticed, but thought it best to let it pass.

At meal's end, Mother instructed Sister to put away the leftovers then retired to take her tea on the porch where she could admire the lacy patterns as the sun filtered through the slender fingers of the pin maple leaves.

Left to herself inside the kitchen, Sister devoured everything that remained of the roast pork. First she sucked the crisp crust, Mother had used a heavy hand with the garlic, then her fingers tore into the deep brown flesh. Leaning over the platter in the center of the kitchen table, she stuffed first one fist-full and then a second into her mouth. Chewing only enough to allow herself to swallow, she crammed in another fistful and then another. Grease dribbled from the corners of her mouth and down behind the bib of her apron onto the front of her Sunday best dress. Sister paid no attention. Pulling the platter closer to her, she ate and ate and ate until nothing remained of the roast. Complaining of a tummy ache, she spent the remainder of the day in her room curled up beneath the quilt with Mary and her frisky lamb.

Later that week, they ate pork chops for supper. Sister said nothing when Mother limited her to one, but late that evening she crept silently down the stairs. Carefully, quietly she removed the glass container of cold leftovers from the refrigerator and carried it to her room. There, under the cover of the quilt, she finished off the chops.

By Christmas Mother had let out Sister's waists and moved the buttons on her shirts. By spring a new wardrobe from Miss Chubby Fashions hung in a neat row in her closet. By fall she'd grown another size still.

At school they noted a change. Now Sister spent her class hours sitting quietly, hands clenched beneath the metal top of her desk, eyes staring absentmindedly at the blackboard. She did no reading, no writing, and no sums. The term's final report suggested Sister be held back. A search of her desk found her assignment papers crumpled together in a pile that somersaulted out onto the floor like oversized kernels from a vendor's popping machine.

In desperation Mother came up with the pig collection idea. They practiced addition and subtraction with rows of little ceramic pigs lined up on the kitchen table. Pink pigs, yellow pigs, red, green, blue and purple pigs. Even one with blue eyes and an outsized daisy clamped between its china teeth.

When by accident, Mother stepped on the blue-eyed pig with the daisy in its mouth, Sister shrieked. Choking with rage, she gathered each broken bit into the safety of her pinafore pocket. Only when Mother finally found the bottle of sticky glue in the back of the hall broom closet did Sister's screams subside long enough to substitute a chip of bone from that evening's barbecued ribs for a missing china leg.

In mending things broken, Sister had found her niche. At home she went on to refashioning broken plates. At school the teachers learned to trade one item needing repair for one lesson paper completed.

With graduation (her sympathetic teachers counted pottery and domestic science twice) Sister found a position as a nurse's aide on the night shift at the senior residence one mile from home. At first the parade of ceramic pigs marched in a perky line along the outer edge of her workstation. Soon, however, the traffic jam of interest they created demanded a move to the round table in the center of the facility's dayroom where the guests could wheel themselves slowly in a circle as they made their selection of the particular pig whose story would be told that day.

Sister delighted in creating a fresh story to go with each pig. Sometimes the braver of the residents told stories of their own. Sometimes the same story bore repeating and repeating until all clamored for the next one. The pig stories mended broken hearts. They prodded disabled limbs into renewed usefulness. Addled brains found new avenues of expression, eyes regained sharper focus, and hands stopped trembling with the exhaustion of lost memories.

Sister, however, declined to tell her own story.

One day an ancient lady accustomed to spending her days alone by a window at the rear corner of the dayroom, wheeled herself painfully over to the center table with its parade of pigs. Round and round she circled the table as if looking for some particular pig. Finally she picked up the blue-eyed pig with the daisy clamped in its china teeth, the one with the bone chip for a leg. Silently, she handed it to Sister then whispered, "Tell me about yours."

Sister stared down at the pig in her hand. She placed it back on the table.

"No, no," a chorus of voices shouted.

Sister took it up again.

"I had a pig," she said. The repressed words gushed out in torrents. "I named her Baby Daisy. Mother had it butchered. I loved that pig so when Sunday dinner came I ate it. Every bit of it. It helped to know that my pig was now a part of me. Fixed things somehow to love it that much. And that's the end."

At first nobody moved. Then one began clapping, then another. Soon a traffic jam developed about the round table with its circle of small china pigs. They were still telling stories when supper time came, and that night everyone went to bed with thoughts of Baby Daisy tucked safely beneath their pillows.

As for Sister, she wiped away a tear with two wads of spring meadow scented tissue. On midnight rounds she pressed into the hand of each of her somnolent charges one small ceramic pig.

"For you to keep," she whispered to those who wakened at her touch. "I don't need them anymore."

THE BLACK WIDOW

A tale of secrets, spiders, and thick stone walls

The truth of it settled long ago into the hidden fissures twisting their way through the red stone walls of an old Pennsylvania farmhouse. The bearer of the tale always tells of a good wife scalded in the overturning of her kettle of boiling laundry. Some claim to know of a horde of black spiders who make covert highway throughout the building. Still others add a row of tiny pine coffins huddled together beneath the planked oak floor of a warm Dutch kitchen.

In the time of William Penn the transplanted Rhinelanders cleared the land of its ancient stands of hard oak and flowering chestnut. They thought first to build the kitchen. Along its north wall they constructed a monstrous fireplace with the dimensions of a room in itself. Therein the housewife's collection of three-legged skillets squatted beside the warm flames like a fraternity of fat black beetles awaiting their arachnidan feast. Above them, projecting at right angles from the fireplace wall, an assemblage of cleverly weighted skewers spiked out over the flagstone hearth. Impaled on the spear points of these long arms a fat roast might slowly sere above the coals, its juices trickling through the sand-filled cracks and down into the narrow dark of the crawl space below.

The heat from the kitchen fire, moving slowly up a curious angle of chimney, exited the house through an ordinary whitewashed brick flue. Barn hands, after their early morning round of icy midwinter chores, tramped into the warm kitchen where they wrapped frosted fingers around generous mugs of steaming cider. Seated on low stools deep in the backmost recesses of the fireplace, they slid their leather boots ever closer into the flames until the shoe tips smoked. Only when the cooks, pinching closed their noses with flour dusted fingers, shouted loud complaints about the odors of the pigsty and the stables would the men remove their offending boots and hang their sodden woolen socks out to dry on the backmost of the skewer's iron arms. Thus the life of the kitchen, redolent with the essence of both barn and bake oven, afforded its tenants the comforts of profound well-being.

On the side of the house farthest removed from the fly ridden cattle pens, stood a deep well from which could be drawn an abundance of fresh water even in the driest of seasons. The overflow from its hand pump, spilling into an ingenious set of enclosed drains, provided the cool stream needed to chill the abundance of the family's fields stored in a cellar beneath the house.

In the shadow of the drains leading to this cold cellar, generations of spiders went about their business while above, in the shade of the porch by the side of the well, the routines of the household's women proceeded apace. In the seclusion of this porch large loaves of bread could be removed from the kitchen's ovens and set out to cool on planks of seasoned oak without the need to fan off green barn flies or chase wandering pigs. On the warmest of days the lazy work of shelling peas, or peeling a mound of potatoes, or rinsing stubborn sand off sweet strawberries could be done in the cool of this ordered retreat beneath the wide porch roof.

This kitchen and its well by the secluded porch, both havens of pure female domesticity, provided the old house with its ghost story. Such is fitting, for it is the women who gave life within the walls of red field stone. It is they who ordered the domestic progression from mother to daughter, from servant to mistress. It is they who dug bare toes into soap drenched mud as they strained to trouble the mass of soiled clothing in the great iron wash kettles. And it is they who, in their dotage seated in the furthest corners of the kitchen fireplace, spindle the rough wool of recall into the thread of organized memory.

Some years after the construction of the house, the growth of the farm's work required an increase in the domestics needed within. No longer could the farmer's wife perform alone all the household's chores. Talk among the local women had it that the daughter of a neighbor, while barely sixteen, could lift the heavy kettles and, if a bit sullen of disposition, had demonstrated competence in baking, and some knowledge of sewing. The housewife spoke to the girl's mother at quilting. One evening a week later the farmer himself strolled down the path by the mill-run to finalize arrangements with the girl's father, whose personal consideration came to a new calf and a good gallon crock of dandelion wine.

The girl assented readily enough. Indeed the entire neighborhood viewed the contract as fortunate for, as the youngest daughter in a large, not especially prosperous family, any arrangements for her future nuptials could offer little beyond a chest filled with the stitchings of her own needle and, if the year proved good, a fat sow with its squalling litter. Although no eligible son graced the family of her new employer, as a servant in a comfortable household she would have ample opportunity to make a way for herself with one or another of the field hands.

So it was settled. Susanna took up residence in the farm house attic near the final bend of the kitchen flue. At the foot of her straw tick rested a rough chest made by the kind hands of her younger brother who knew, with regret, that upon her leaving he would be called upon to tend the chickens and milk the family's single cow. The chest contained only a thin blanket, a worn quilt, and the lace trimmed petticoat which the girl wore under her woolen outer skirt when in attendance at service of a Sabbath morning.

In appearance Susanna curved in the manner of a pleasantly round golden apple, plump from her tight crown of braids to the smooth humps of her ample hips. But for all her country flavor the girl conducted herself with the utmost reserve. Only a trifling tease in the swing of her full skirts vaguely suggested the seeds of trouble to the most observant of women.

In truth, however, Susanna's personal ambitions roved far beyond the limited horizons of the farm hands whose observations focused on such things as rounded hips and what might lie beneath flipped skirts. Susanna privately coveted nothing less than the lavender scented sheets and properly curtained bedstead of her new mistress, the wife of the prosperous farmer in whose kitchen she had consented to labor.

With these vague proddings of ambition tucked beneath the pleats of her demure white cap, Susanna cheerfully began her farmhouse duties in early March. By August, the farmer's wife, now full with child, expressed complete satisfaction with her new serving girl to the women of the church quilting circle, noting that Susanna tended to her work rather than to the glances of the hands. This observation, offered as it was in sincere relief, was seconded by the other ladies who pointed to the girl's surprising habit of ignoring the young men who capered about the tables of lemonade and cookies set out on the church lawn after Sunday worship. For their part these country swains, puzzled at Susanna's aloofness, soon resorted to betting on which of their amorous wiles might win her briefest glance.

The winter months went by in this manner. On the first of April the farmer's wife gave birth to a robust baby boy. Not one to linger long in the confinement customary for new mothers, she resumed her household duties two weeks later. On one particularly lovely morning as the farm hands prepared for spring plowing, the good wife first nursed the new baby. She then assisted Susanna with getting the men off with lunch baskets of sausage, fried potatoes and shoo-fly pie for the long day behind their teams. After which the wife directed her serving girl to gather wood and the dirty clothing and to place the heavy kettles so they might be more easily filled with water for the laundry. Susanna, however, complained of a slight malaise.

Desiring to be far along in her labors before the child again required her breast, the housewife herself proceeded with the wash while the girl continued with the lighter tasks of the kitchen.

The large iron kettles in which the soiled field clothes were boiled rested on the grass on the far side of the well by the secluded porch. From the woodshed the good wife brought an armful of split pine and small branches, from the kitchen a shovel-full of hot coals. Soon the fire crackled brightly. The iron kettles brimmed to overflowing as the woman stirred soft soap shavings and then the dirty laundry into the rapidly heating caldrons.

On this particular morning after a rain during the night, the earth underfoot, always sodden by the end of washday, had become uncommonly slippery. But the housewife, her hands busy with the laundry and her mind with thoughts of preparations for the evening meal, dismissed the slick as a nuisance. A single yellow flame licking out from under the pots reminded her to tuck up her skirts under her belt. She deposited her wooden clogs by the side of the stone porch and, her bare toes providing a firmer grip, proceeded with her work. As she waited for the fire to heat the water further, the woman made frequent side trips to the kitchen to check on the baby. During one such diversion she advised Susanna to run off to the other side of the orchard to cut the spring's best red rhubarb for the evening's cobbler.

The baby's awakening movements hastened the mother's desire to finish the wash now steaming in earnest over an intense blaze. She took in hand the great paddle with which to agitate the clothing. Bending far forward, she plunged the paddle into the depths of the caldron and with great effort pulled toward her a heavy twisting of stiff overalls and stained work shirts.

At that moment, losing their grip on the moss, her bare feet skidded out from under her. The wooden stirring paddle to which she clung tipped the kettle, unleashing a torrent of boiling water. Fearfully scalded, one leg pinned under the overturned kettle, the good wife could not move. A loud shriek, then a second, and finally, mercifully, the black of unconsciousness.

Out beyond the orchard Susanna heard the screams. Dropping her full basket she ran to the house. There she found the baby howling in distress and her mistress lying unconscious beneath the wet tangle of steaming clothes. Instinctively Susanna moved to assist her mistress, but as she bent over to do so, she stopped. A slight smile coiled at the corners of her mouth.

Turning her back on the disaster, Susanna returned to the kitchen where she picked up the baby, changed the child and pacified it with some honey on the tip of her finger. Only after the child quieted did she attempt to assist her moribund mistress.

The frantic toiling of the barnyard's alarm bell summoned the hands from the far fields. Speechless in face of the horror of it, the men carried the unconscious woman up the winding back stair to her lavender-scented bed where neighbor women had gathered to attend her. Susanna, the track of her tears marking plain passage down an exceptionally high rose in her cheeks, sat by a cold kitchen hearth rocking the baby. The farmer, so resourceful in other matters, stood by his wife's bedside wringing his hands. Shuffling from one foot to the other, eyes downcast, his male friends assembled about the trestle table in the great room. Speechless, they clutched their battered felt hats before them, then left at dusk to milk the grieving farmer's herd and round up his hogs. Two went off to construct a coffin that by unspoken consensus all agreed would be needed by morning.

The next evening, his wife laid to rest in the family plot out behind Wentz's Church, the great room's trestle table laden to groaning under the outpouring of dishes from the kitchens of every neighbor, the farmer sat down to a solitary meal. Susanna, taking the baby down the road to her own mother's home for the night, first fed the child warm goat's milk and then lay down on her childhood's mattress of ticked straw. A candle, guttering in the draft from a tear in the oiled paper covering the window, cast little moving patterns on the rafters close above her head. Once again a smug smile snatched at the corners of her mouth. At peace, she extinguished the flame.

A farmer must have a capable wife, especially in the summer when the labor in the fields demands many hands needing to be fed from a generous kitchen. Accordingly, the farmer speedily took unto himself a new helpmate. Since she was available and possessed a good knowledge of the kitchen, the farmer married Susanna, the serving girl who had been so faithful in her care of his now motherless child.

This rapid, but not altogether unexpected, turn of events prompted only a snippet of comment on the good fortune of the younger daughter of the farmer's poor neighbor. Despite the press of their own household duties, the women of the community bustled about to piece the intertwined rings of a new quilt for the still empty dower chest which Susanna had brought with her when first employed. Life in the stone farmhouse proceeded on into the end of the harvest.

With dignity befitting her elevated status, Susanna assumed charge of the household. Assisted by a newly hired girl, she laid a bountiful table. Indeed, the opportunity for a taste of her light corn puddings, a mouthful of her sweet succotash, or a slice of her thick apple pie persuaded many a man to hire on for field work at wages somewhat lower than those generally offered at surrounding farms. Susanna herself took great care to act in the manner of a properly married woman. Not a breath of scandal breezed from the conversations about her table. The younger hands turned their attentions to the new serving girl, whose appearance and general demeanor engendered less interest than that of her mistress while serving at that very table scarcely a season past.

The farmer's baby son thrived on a generous supply of goat's milk, and the sympathetic stitchings of the neighbor wives ensured that he took his first steps fully outfitted as his late, lamented mother would have wished. Indeed, by the end of the next harvest season no more tranquil domestic scene was to be found in the entire township. The laces on her bodice having tightened and the girth of her waist having thickened, Susanna increased in a maternal way. Word passed among the women that the birth could be expected in the dead of winter just after the turn of the new year.

One day as the first frosts of October bit into the pumpkins and a young winter wind rattled the long leaves on the drying corn stalks, Susanna descended the steps into the cold cellar. Along the basement walls stood crock after crock filled with the season's pickled cucumbers and spiced fruit. A cool stream of water from the well's overflow trickled across the carved stone tub in which yesterday's butter hardened, and thick cream formed a rich cap on pails of sweet milk.

Susanna surveyed the scene with satisfaction. Her larder, as indeed her life, overflowed. The same smug smile as on the momentous night of her mistress' death pulled once more at the corners of her mouth.

Turning to fetch a cutting of soap from the block stored by the deep window well, Susanna spied a trio of black spiders making their accustomed way down along the edge of the drain. She moved to crush the beasts with her shoe. The spiders, as if anticipating her attack, jumped into her skirts and lost themselves in the flounces of her full petticoats.

More annoyed than frightened, Susanna shook her skirts with vigor. With their swish there came from the cracks in the great stone foundation of the cellar the strangest breeze, a low moan as if the structure itself had sucked in its breath. Startled, the young woman turned toward the stairs only to find her way blocked by the floating form of her former mistress clad in the long woolen cloak in which she had been wrapped when so early laid to rest in her grave. The apparition's eyes possessed a piercing energy. The hair, which in life had hung in a long, thick braid down her back, now stood straight out from the naked skull. With a shriek not unlike those that twisted with the north wind up the bend of the old chimney, the ghost faded back into the dark crawl space beneath the kitchen.

Susanna fainted.

Attributing the young woman's indisposition to the delicacies of growing motherhood, the midwife prescribed bed rest and generous cups of warm beef broth. But Susanna, craving the company of the others about the house, betook herself to the comforts of a pillowed Windsor chair which her husband set out for her under a large maple so that she might enjoy the mild breezes of the golden Indian summer. Seated there, the needles in her fingers flew as she knitted little garments for her infant who would enter this world in the biting cold of the coming January.

The autumnal red of the maple, the heavenly blue of the sky, and the rich orange of the pumpkins piled by the adjacent woodshed so beguiled, that the incident of the spiders in the basement and the ghost by its narrow stairwell retreated to the inner recesses of her mind. So completely inattentive did she become that Susana failed to note the trio of black spiders that slipped noiselessly down from her skirts back into the hidden reaches of the crawl space beneath the kitchen.

As January's birthing day approached, deep snow wrapped the entire countryside in one of those frozen white blankets which hold both men and beast close beside the warmth of well-tended fires. The midwife, whose slow trek through the waist-high drifts had robbed her of breath and set a high rose on the cheeks of the lad sent to fetch her, arrived at the moment of the presentation of the baby's head. Beside the tight twist of the umbilical cord around the neck of the child blazed a raised welt, the mark imprinted as if the infant had been bitten in utero. The child, uttering a single feeble cry, expired.

Assisted by the serving girl, the midwife washed the mother and, after giving her a potion to enhance sleep, prepared the infant's body for burial. Sorrowing, the farmer made a small coffin from woodshed scraps. This he lined tightly with tin, for the frigid inclemency of the weather rendered impossible the completion of a proper burial. He would, therefore, be forced to store the securely sealed body of his baby in the crawl space beneath the loose oaken planks of the old kitchen floor. That sad task completed, he seated himself on the low chair kept in the far corner of the huge fireplace, a mug of hot gruel in hand. Between long sips of his drink he observed to the midwife seated beside him that the spot in which he had laid the babe's coffin seemed strangely to have been swept clear of the dust that elsewhere had settled in a thick mantle across the narrow space beneath the busy kitchen above. At this observation a gust of the north wind shrieked down the chimney, his toddler son fled to his lap, and a procession of spiders retreated unobserved deep into the long crevice above the wrought iron skewers.

Susanna soon rose from her bed to resume the care of the house and of the first wife's child, who by now ran freely about the kitchen directly above the resting place of the small wooden box which held the remains of his half brother. Susanna tended this child as her own so that he continued to grow stout of body and sweet of disposition. As she cared for the child, she cared for her house and for those who lived therein. Her larder was full. The warmth of her ovens supplied the table with the most delicious of breads. Not a suggestion of tarnish bedimmed her pewter plates, and the evening flight of her fingers as they twirled her spindle or clicked her needles furnished the family with clothing of estimable quality.

Only one circumstance interrupted the serendipitous progression of the seasons. Each year, hard after the festivity of the Christ's birth, Susanna would be delivered of an infant. The strange particulars of these confinements were identical. A hard snow and deep cold would occasion the midwife's tardy arrival. The babe would present strangled in the umbilical cord, the raised red welt of a bite flamed on its neck. The sealed casket would take its place in the crawl space beneath the kitchen floor. All those present would clench their teeth against the wild howl of the wind down the tortured length of the kitchen chimney. Even when warmer weather thawed the frozen ground, Susanna would not permit the small boxes enclosing the remains of her children to be removed for proper burial from the crawl space beneath where she worked each day. So as the years progressed, the row of little coffins snuggled together in silent sleep grew longer, and still longer. Those who worked beside her in the kitchen and those who ate so well at her table noted, however, a gradually increasing aspect of unnatural gray which spread further over their mistress' visage with each January's unfortunate delivery.

Noted too were the deepening furrows carving themselves into her countenance so lately smooth and full-fleshed. The alteration in her appearance proved so profound as to etch the deepest lines of advanced age into her features by the age of twenty and nine. Likewise, her once golden hair turned from its youthful crown of braided glory to split strings of yellowed white pulled into a parsimonious bun at the nape of her neck. Her choice of clothing, from its initial bedecking with the lighter hues of youth, first turned several shades darker and then to an exhausted black just a tone darker than the depleted aspect of her skin.

The cellar remained as cold as it had been on that day when Susanna fainted at the sight of the ghost of her former mistress. The serving girls, for the household by now employed two of them, reported brushing great spiders back into their clandestine lair beneath the kitchen whenever they descended the steps to fork pickles out of the crock or to cut soap from the basket by the window. Susanna herself visited the cellar only infrequently, and then only in the company of others.

Increasingly the labors of the kitchen, the collection of stores against the winter, and the multitude of duties so common to the housewife were given into the capable hands of those in her employ. Her hair now unkempt, her clothing disheveled, Susanna busied herself at her spindle twisting combed wool into yarn for her knitting. So gradual had been the transformation of her visage, so completely had her humor been bound by the strict regimen of grief, so able was her husband to provide for the household, that none in the community thought to suspect the real basis of her profound indisposition. None but Susanna knew of her deliberate failure to help on that long ago day when her mistress met her untimely end.

One day in the usual storm of a bitter January as the northwest wind cried once more down the bend in the chimney, the new bride of the old farmer's only son took her corn husk broom to the fine gray ash swirled across her scrubbed kitchen floor by the force of the storm without. By the edge of the great fireplace, she stopped. There on the hearth before her she spied a great spider.

At that very moment a renewed blast of cold wind moaned down the chimney. The coals on the hearth blazed into flame. As the bent form of Susanna struggled to rise from her stool in the furthest reaches of the fireplace, the great spider, its long black legs waving in rhythm, made determined advance up over the old crone's black cape to her neck. Swiftly, deliberately, its sharp fangs pierced the sagging flesh.

That evening, those in attendance on the corpse noted with some puzzlement the peculiar redness of the ugly welt raised by the swift bite of the spider. None could recall a similar incision at the jugular, except, of course, the miniature punctures burned into the neck of each of Susanna's dead babes.

The cold of January having, as usual, frozen the earth to uncommon depth, Susanna was laid to rest beside the long row of little coffins beneath the oak plank floor of the kitchen. Promptly, however, with the first warmth of spring, the young farmer set out to move all the coffins to the comfort of the family plot in the burial ground by Wentz's Church.

Lifting aside the floorboards his workmen found the small caskets of the children complete as they should be, but the box holding Susanna's remains had in the space of four short months been transformed into a great white sacque of finely woven threads. Uneasy, the farmhands attempted to scrape away the mass from the coffin with the flat blades of their spades. Forthwith there spewed out from the web a host of miniature black spiders who promptly retreated into the myriad passageways in the stone foundation of the house. The hands' misdirected blows shattered the wood of the box into a scatter of splinters that mingled with a foul effluent pouring from a gash in the coffin's tin lining. Gagging, the workmen refused to proceed. It was left to the young farmer to rake unaided his stepmother's putrefied bones into a tote of rough burlap.

And so, Susanna's remains found a final resting place, not beside the plot of her husband or near the small stones which marked the graves of their children, but under the black thorn bush which still grows in wild profusion out beyond the churchyard fence. And though more than a century has since sped by, today's custodian of Wentz's white-steepled church solemnly advises due respect for the hex alive in the mere prick of those same malevolent thorns.

And the present inhabitants of the old house find it wise to caution any child dispatched to the cold cellar to retrieve a jar of green beans for the evening's meal. The warning not to linger is stern for if one should turn of a sudden toward the heavy coats and red wool mufflers rowed on their pegs along the stairs, the chances are real of a momentary encounter with the black-cloaked ghost from long-ago. Indeed it is averred that when the fierce north wind howls down the crook in the old chimney the voice heard is that of the old farmer's first wife screaming in her distress.

And, as has been their timeless custom, the current generation of spiders continues to make its secret way through the hidden cracks that labyrinth throughout the thick stone walls of the old Dutch farmhouse.

LORD'S DAY GOTHIC

A wife, a husband,
cinnamon buns, and blue jays

Their Sunday routine:

Zipped tightly into a long blue houserobe, she comes downstairs first. Turning the lock on the kitchen door, she bends to pick up the single quart of milk the dairy has left in the entryway. Greeting the three cats, she offers them scraps from the evening's meal. A young squirrel sits, tail flicking in expectant familiarity, on the edge of the low rock wall. She admonishes him to wait his turn, then inspects the bird feeder, and the robin's nest almost hidden in the maple's new green. Finding all in order, she returns to her kitchen.

A shuffle of feet on the front landing signals his descent from the bedroom to his study. There, in the midst of a grand disorder of scattered paper and weighty statute books, he turns to earnest labor over the composition of wills and the fine points in legal briefs. Such is his discipline. Wills and fine points, the legalities.

With the sounds of his stirring, she turns to the preparation of breakfast. This day, the Lord's Day, commands a particular ritual, a routine dug solidly into the foundation of fifty wedded years. Always they begin with a breakfast of cinnamon buns, the fat Philadelphia kind lavished with brown sugar syrup, walnuts, raisins and maraschino cherries.

She purchases them each Friday after her hair appointment in Germantown. Hilda, the scrubbed German girl behind the counter, always knots each delicacy securely into its plain white box. Hilda even offers assistance to the car. "You carry this little one. I will get the rest," she says. And they pause a moment to chat in the sunshine by the side of the car, until the meter runs out and her customer hastily departs in a flurry of inchoate personal incrimination.

When the children had been home she would have emerged from Hebner's bakery with a baker's dozen and quite likely a cheese cake as well. Now with the children gone, one box of a half dozen provides more than enough for the Sunday couple of them. She thinks of their sons this morning as she lifts the cardboard lid. David and Jonathan. A swift glance checks again the date of David's impending visit marked in bold on her household calendar. Just the thought of the full box on hand for him the weekend after next sends a warm pulse through her whole being. David always finds an excuse to eat at least one large bun as soon as he steps into the kitchen. Her ears strain for the sound of his tires on the gravel, the pop as he tears through the tape on the side of the bakery box, the satisfied smack as he licks the remaining drips of sticky syrup from the edges of his mouth.

With a sigh she turns to the day at hand, lays out places for two at the kitchen table. His, as always, at the head and hers, as always, to the side next to the stove from where she can jump up to serve him quickly. She fills the kettle with fresh water for her instant coffee and pours a glass of skimmed milk for him.

Preparations completed, she waits. As she waits she empties last night's dishes from the washer. Dusting off imagined specks, she places each plate in its proper spot in her ample cupboards. For a second time she runs a wet rag over the counter tops. He lingers still in his study. She sighs, glances at the kitchen wall clock and turns down the burner under the kettle. That he has never been conscious of her waiting, of her small, time-filling rituals, she knows, but excuses as his absorption in his work, his need for uninterrupted time to think.

"Good Morning," represents the extent of his greeting.

With a jerk he pulls his chair from the table, reciting as he sits down the same one-line grace his father chanted in identical manner before him. She has barely taken her seat when he begins the litany. At the mumbled *Amen* she springs to her feet to pour her coffee and retrieve two warm buns from the toaster oven.

"The day is a lovely one," she begins. "The squirrel covets the cats' food and I believe there are three blue eggs in the robins' nest."

"You and your cats," he says.

"Two weeks and David will be here." Delicately, she holds the largest maraschino cherry for a moment on her tongue.

"I believe Jonathan's Sue may be expecting again," she smiles.

"How do you know? You've not been told."

"Just a feeling." She smiles again, the secret smile of women who know.

"Jonathan cannot support the ones they have," he says. "Situations such as his come to no good. A very poor marriage, but then it wasn't up to me. He never would take my advice."

"They're looking for a house, a bigger one." She picks the hard walnut pieces from the caramel topping, pushes them to the side of her plate.

"Where will they get the money? Poor planning, no thought." He speaks through a mastication of dough and nuts. Bits of two cherries fall out of his mouth. Butter dribbles down his chin.

She glances once again at the wall clock and then at him. "It's nine-thirty. The service begins at eleven."

"I need more time with a brief," he mumbles and returns again to his study.

The clock chimes ten-thirty. Hat in place, gloves on, she seats herself in the living room. He emerges from his study still in his pajamas, the oversized ones with the long droop in the drawers and a narrow dangle of tape in the front.

"Get the car," he orders as he turns to go up the stairs. Automatically, she rises to comply.

They rush down their narrow country road at fifty-five miles per hour. He allots stop signs the merit of cursory attention and favors the graveled back roads.

"Less traffic, fewer officers," he says and then repeats the line more emphatically as if daring the sheriff's attention.

She nods dutifully, knows his script as well as he.

A slight smile of private pleasure flits across her face.

"Mildred and I went to the Audubon house the other day," she says. "The historical society folks have restored the place. It is most attractive. I purchased the new folio, ten prints. We could put two over our beds."

He swerves around a corner, pulls hard left to avoid a pothole. "We should sue for these roads," he mutters. "They raise taxes and they raise taxes. We have to put up with this state of the highways. It's downright criminal. You'll need to take the car for realignment on Tuesday."

"Tuesday is my day at the nursing home. They count on me." She frowns, turns to look at him.

"I have to have it first thing Wednesday," he says.

"Can't it wait until Thursday?" Her voice sinks to a whisper.

"Try to organize yourself." He snorts, pumps at the brake then speeds through a light.

"Very well," she replies.

They walk into the sanctuary as the congregation stands for the mid-service hymn. An usher motions them toward a center pew. She finds the page and hands him the hymnal. Her finger indicates the last verse of *Onward Christian Soldiers*. At rigid attention, he monotones his version of the words. She sings on tune, true to the text. During the sermon she keeps a finger beneath the lines in the pew Bible. He jots dollar signs and jumbles of numbers in the margins of the program bulletin. At the benediction he rises, pushes his way in front of her to station himself under the vestibule's stained glass window. Standing there, smile on ready, he extends his hand toward every business opportunity.

She remains in her pew, greets her neighbor, arranges for the ladies' sewing circle on Friday, and hears that Mrs. Wright who has played the Sunday School piano for thirty years had fallen ill in the night. Young Joseph, son of their Jonathan, the mischievous redheaded one with the fine ear for music, had taken over at the piano that morning. He had done so well. She makes sure to tell him how splendid a substitute he had made and how she regrets that they had not been there to hear.

They step out the church door as the sexton turns the old iron key.

She has to hurry as he strides across the parking lot in parade double time.

She takes his arm, attempts to draw him into step with her, tells him about Joseph and how well he had done.

"Perhaps he will go into music. He has talent." Her eyes beam with pride.

"Certainly not," he retorts. "Don't give him any of your crazy ideas."

"You promised him a weekend in New York City for his birthday. He's checked out Web sites for the Statue of Liberty, and Carnegie Hall. I've purchased tickets for a concert at Carnegie Hall." She glances tentatively in his direction.

"Tell him to add the Stock Exchange and be sure the concert is classical. None of this hopping jazz he gets into." He shakes her hand from his arm, beeps open their car.

They lunch at a country restaurant, by a picture window overlooking a pond where a mother duck shepherds her young.

"Look," she says, "seven little ones for that mother to guide into the water. Their nest must be hidden by the willow."

Beyond the pond, trucks buzz by on a major highway, beyond that a cluster of new houses, and in the distance beyond the houses, the white cone of a nuclear reactor rises above freshly harrowed fields.

"How sad," she sighs.

He snorts, "First you are out to make a wimp of that boy and now you're worried about pollution. You have no sense at all. Musicians starve and reactors lower utility bills. It is as simple as that."

He eats *Jell-O*, strawberry with pears. She chooses the salad bar and goes to make her selection. Back at the table again, she settles herself, opens her napkin.

"They have five bean salad on the menu today," she beams.

"Why you like it, I cannot understand." He gulps around a mouth full of pear, swallowed whole. "Must be something genetic in that Dutch farm background of yours."

"The *Jell-O* looks good, but I make it all the time at home."

Carefully, she positions five beans on her fork, brings them to her lips and smiles as she tastes. "They blend so nicely," she says with a wise look in his direction. Shifting slightly in her seat, she prays heavenly forgiveness for that look. That soundless, delicate act of defiance-in-miniature. That diminutive slip from her accustomed acquiescence.

Their entrees come, baked chicken with mashed potatoes and bright new peas.

"Delicious," she says. "It can be hard to cook peas well."

"I like them out of the can, soft so they mash with my fork," he growls. "You always have to eat something different. Just give me the usual."

As they eat she watches the ducks, hums to herself a line from the morning's hymn, compliments the waitress on the chicken, and accepts another glass of iced tea. They order plain vanilla ice cream for dessert.

"Skimped on the scoops," he growls, then pays the bill in cash, leaves a two-dollar tip.

She slips an additional bill under her napkin. As they rise to leave she nods in appreciation toward the waitress.

Back at home she retires to their bedroom for an afternoon nap and he to his study to read. In fact he sleeps. She knows he will. Her rest quickly over, she creeps down the back stairs and makes her way out to the meadow to walk through the blue bottles and wild tulips massed about the old spring house. The cats follow her to the meadow gate then sit by its posts licking their paws until her return.

In the late afternoon, he joins her on the porch where they snack on chocolate covered marshmallows.

"Someone has been into my chocolates. Keep a closer watch on Emma." He removes the empty papers and counts those remaining.

"Seven," he says.

With nightfall, they move inside. Standing by the kitchen counter he wolfs down what remains of the cinnamon buns. She deposits the empty bakery box in the trash, then carries the full sack out to the woodshed. He settles himself in the living room, selects a book from the stack on the carpet by his chair. She gets out her needlepoint, searches for her glasses. So many fine stitches require a special pair.

Her needle moves in and out as he talks about the government. The Democrats are ruining the country. He plans an injunction to halt power company expansion. Humming quietly she works an iris in subtle blues. Occasionally she holds her canvas up at arm's length and with a squint checks the blend of color. She asks for his response.

"About the same as your last one," he says.

"They are a pair, but not alike," she replies. "I worked the other in ten shades of pink."

"Why don't you show some imagination," he grunts.

At nine they retire to twin beds. She turns down each spread, smoothes each pillow, then creeps between her covers.

"As soon as I'm able I'll have the Audubons framed. Would you like the blue jays over your bed?" she asks.

BEGGARS' FEAST

Midnight in the cathedral

At *Señora* Theresa's tiny *posada* the rooms sparkle, the showers run hot, and she leaves fresh lemons in the basket below Our Lady's small shrine on the wall outside my door. Peeled open their bite sustains me through *Señora's* midmorning summary of the day's news.

"America! Violent," she intones. "Dangerous. Young people drunk and into sex. Godless." *Señora* crosses herself twice before Our Lady's shrine at the entrance to my room. "Go to the cathedral," she tells me. "Go to mass like a good girl. Wear something to cover your arms." Dismissing me with a wave, she returns to her daily scrubbings of steps.

Señora's prescriptions weary me, but I give in. "Okay, if you say so, *Señora* Teresa." Knit tops with spaghetti straps, no bra, define the real me. However, to humor her, I will go to the cathedral wearing my single shirt with long sleeves, the cuffs buttoned properly at the wrist.

Señora Theresa assumes I'm wandering, like the rest of the student-traveler generation whose boots leave black scuffs on her marble steps. In truth religion has more to do with other people's stories than it does with my immediate realities. But, deep down, I'm wary lest somehow I end up entrapped in tradition's insidious web after all.

Clamping on my hat, settling my glasses securely on the bridge of my nose, I wave at the cat sleeping in the shade of the lemon tree and make for the street.

Soon I'm totally lost in a maze of dark medieval alleys. A young woman, hair spiked electric purple, eyes me from her seat in the recess of an ancient doorway. Her left hand moves round and round massaging spindly legs with a mixture of cold cream and brown goo.

Tossing a ten *peseta* coin into her cup, I request direction to the main square.

"*Allá.*" Pale blue eyes bore at me through long black lashes. The slight hitch of her head motioning me toward a narrow passageway dislodges the shawl draped about her shoulders, revealing a stump where a right arm should be. Its ugly protuberance of pulpy flesh flaps irritably as if silently determined to swat me full in the face.

I recoil. She laughs. A low gurgle of a laugh, a cynical grieving angst as brown as the mud she mixes with that glob of cold cream.

"*¡Vete!*" Throwing my condescending coin back at my feet, she motions me gone.

The alley twists open onto a vast cathedral square where the full power of a merciless midday sun speeds my way toward the church. Once inside I slide onto a bench beneath the intersection of the great main vaults. Behind and beside me parades a regiment of Romanesque columns. Before me a scatter of pilgrims mutters responses as an aged priest muddles his way through the usual incantations.

Sunlight shafts from high clerestory windows. From far aloft a trail of incense clouds the sacramental table. Sweet wisps of myrrh and cloves encircle the shaking hands of a tiny lady who chants the routine of service in a manner as precise as the placement of her starched lace collar.

A teenage couple crowds beside me on the bench. She's all hyperactive snickers, high leather boots, and a mere scrap of a mini skirt. Admiring the widening fissure between the top of the boots and the hem of her clothing, he whispers. She giggles.

The little lady hisses an indignant, "*¡Cállense!*"

Silence restored, I take off my glasses, carefully position them in their case, and place them in the rack beside the missal.

Incense lazes still lower. The waxy scent of the warm votives intoxicates. I close my eyes to look, tentatively, inward.

But not for long. An elbow jabs my side. Mini Skirt will partake of the elements, a grace she undoubtedly could use. I rise to let her pass, then move forward myself. Following the tap of her electric green boots, I face the priest who stifles a yawn as he dips the wafer, peering at me through rheumy eyes as he places it on my tongue. This pasty version of the body of Our Lord glues itself to my tongue.

Directly the rumble of an empty stomach propels me out into the open air. Forgetful of my wire rims nestled in their case by the missal, I dig sunglasses out of my fanny pack and walk across the open square in search of something more substantial than manufactured biscuit for lunch. Reality has its immediacies. Accordingly, I find a café. Alone at a tiny table tucked into a window well, I feast on pimentos stuffed with crab, olives from a deep barrel, an aged cheese, and hot bread in thick slices with crusts that crunch on the teeth. A tumbler filled to brimming from one of those bottles of cheap red wine washes all down.

When I assure her that I have indeed been to mass, *Señora* Teresa adds a plump orange to the dish of lemons by my bed. She pats my hand, promises to crochet a lace edge to my shirt collar, and asks if I'd like a bit on the cuffs too.

After the obligatory siesta, I leave my long-sleeved shirt for *Señora*, waiting by my door with her cotton and hook. She smiles satisfaction when I compliment her on the sweetness of her orange.

Now it is late afternoon. Friends from yesterday urge me back to the sweeping expanse of plaza fronting the cathedral. I wish to hunt at once for my wire rims, but they insist my dark lenses will do to experience the glory of the evening's blaze as it ennobles the great west windows of the church.

"It is said," they read from a guidebook, "that medieval pilgrims, glimpsing from afar the heavenly luster of these very windows, knew that the path that had worn to shreds the thick leather soles of their sandals had come to an end, believing in this holy place the weary traveler could finally step within a hair's space of a saint."

The bones of a saint at least.

A tiny dog in a yellow tutu dances a jig before the church steps. He has help from a little boy who runs about collecting small coins from tourists who stare at the dog. One pleads in a shrill voice for one more photo opportunity because she's failed to advance her film. Beneath the thick arbor of the *parador* my friends and I sip coffee, three sugars, as we conjure up the thousands who will crowd the square on *El Día de Santiago*. Together we sophisticate over the perfectly balanced architecture, the intricately patterned stones of the pavement. We bask in these rosy technicalities until I recall witches, not to mention Jewish merchants, roasted here in the Inquisition's bonfires from hell.

My companions laugh, pound my back, tell me to ignore the charred remains of history. "Lighten up and live for today," they preach. Linking arms they escort me to the bars for repeated draughts of appropriate fortification. "Cheers and long life," they sing.

At the hour before midnight the measured tones of the heavy bronze bells of the great church jolt awake the gathering of pigeons nested at the base of the clock tower. The reverberation ripples the surface of the last deep cup in front of me. My head reels. My ears pound with the unrelenting beat of the bells.

The effect of the cup.

We began with my morning trip to the cathedral where I left my glasses without which my view of the world blurs at the edges. My rush to exit for lunch. Now it is nearing midnight. I am driven to stumble my way back to the cathedral.

The bartender's eyebrows bush in alarm when I tell him where I must go. "*Señorita*, hear me. This is not wise, alone in the dark and you have had much to drink."

I insist.

With a shrug he tells me of a small door to the cathedral. "In a recess to the left of the street lamp. It is never locked. Stay in the shadows on this side of the street. Take care that the *Guardia* has passed before you enter."

It is no trouble to find the little door. I run my fingers over its wood, trace the thick iron studs, tug the leather thong at the latch, venture a tentative push. The door swings silently inward. All the ghosts captive within swish out with the escaping blast of chill interior air. They twist at my clothing, stand my hair on end, whistle about my ears. I pull my jacket collar up to my chin and step cautiously inward.

I stumble toward a red glow floating at waist height a dozen paces before me. A brazier banked for the night. Near it there is a breath, the slow pulse of deep slumber. I pause, my torso rigid, poised for flight. With one hand before me groping, the other squeezed into my jacket pocket, I move forward reassuring myself that I am fully sober, wholly engaged in a simple mission of reconnection with my lost glasses. Indeed as I shuffle forward, I pride myself on my detached composure as I move into the transepts.

The flickering line of votives guides me toward the altar. From there I make the left turn down the side aisle to my seat of the morning. I finger my way past the dark mass of a column. I grope for the backs of benches, one, two, then three, four, finally five. Finding the bench, I carefully slip toward its center. I reach for the rack, for my glasses, and they are there. Not on end in their case as I remember, but lengthwise along the base of the rack. Someone has moved them so. Perhaps to make room for the missal. But no, the missal is gone. Perhaps my glasses fell of their own accord when the book was removed. No matter. My task complete, I relax. Mechanically I remove the wire frames from their case, adjust the ear pieces, fix the narrow rims high on my nose.

Satisfied, I lean back on my seat. Once more my world takes on sharp lines, definite edges. The great bell on the clock tower begins the midnight hour. At that moment, a spark of gold glints from the crowns of the stone saints. An unsteady flame walks slowly to a spot before the altar. Then another. And yet another. In the tiny radiance the line of stoic marble effigies high above me in their narrow wall niches seem to move. Silk robes to flow. Elongated fingers to bend. Fixed pupils to pulse. Wide-eyed they stare down at me as I crouch on the hard planks of the worshipers' bench.

And there is more: a stir, a whisper, a low laugh. To my right, to my left more shadows approach. Not with the smooth glide of a newly engendered spirit, but halting to the hunch and tap of a crutch. They pass within a step of my pew, each bringing a light to the altar. Candle stubs cradled in rusted tin cans. Discarded pottery shards. A small congregation seats itself on the stone floor before the altar.

One draws a long loaf of bread from a roll of newsprint. "From the baker," they say with a low laugh. "The old cheat, too crippled to give chase. Always blesses with the richest of language."

A jar of olives appears from a coat pocket. "The grocer," another announces. "Just walked right in and helped myself right in front of him. He blesses with a yell too as he stands close guard over his cash register."

A block of cheese. A great knife driven into it. "From the sisters. They give with the sign of the cross, and strict admonition to remember to return their knife," chuckles another.

"Where is the wine? Where is she with the wine? On the street this morning she had a bottle beneath her blanket. She's maybe drunk it all herself."

Another laugh. A stir, and then a new light gleams from behind the high altar. The gold in the elevated crown of the patron saint dances as an arm, long, lean, and beautifully formed, encircles the neck of James son of Zebedee, *Santiago,* follower of the Christ. Slowly, one by one the white tips of a sculptor's fingers caress the jewels in his crown.

"She's here," they whisper.

Patiently, they wait. Finally a single flame descends from the saint's high place. It glints purple off short spiked hair. The stride flows smoothly. The robe is white.

I clamp my hands hard along the edge of my bench. Driblets of perspiration track uneven paths across my scalp.

Holding the bottle high, she descends to the circle before the altar. Her congregation moves toward her. "You save any for us, or drink it all yourself?" They laugh.

She pours into the vessels thrust forward; a plastic tumbler, a chipped dish, a crushed paper cup.

For each an equal portion. Held close, their candles examine every drop.

The pouring completed, she faces my direction. "There is a stranger here," she says into the darkness. "Come. There is enough."

I feel for my wallet. Find it secure inside my inner pouch.

"Come," they say again. "We watched you enter through the priest's door. You nearly fell over Pedro here who sleeps by the brazier. They give him space on the floor by the fire. Watches the place for them, he does. Come along now. Join us."

Slowly, I make my way to the circle.

The one who stands to the side saddles up close. In a pulse of malodorous breath he tells me to call him Judas.

"No need to hide yourself or your wallet down the left leg of those fancy blue jeans you wear. We are gentlemen in this house," he says.

"Saw you drag that wallet out this morning when you made that phone call by the square," adds another.

"Likely it would buy us all a fine dinner," they grin in chorus through a troop of pitted teeth.

Pedro rises, grips my arm. Whispers that he'd found my glasses but didn't need them himself; besides, things that turned up in the house of the Lord didn't fit in his pockets. With a low tickle of a laugh, he pushes me to a seat on the altar step.

"Afraid of us, ain't you," they chortle. We would harass you if it weren't here in this place and time for bread and wine. And tonight, to sweeten the whole, olives with cheese."

I sit among them, a crisp crust from their proffered loaf clutched close-fisted in my hand.

Then the beautiful arm reaches toward me. She hands me her cup. "You gave me ten *pesetas* this morning, Sister," she says. "Thanks. But, make it one hundred tomorrow."

A bent figure at my left pokes at me with his cane. "Name's Tomas," he says. "Believe, and tomorrow remember to give her one hundred so she can bribe the clerk at the medical clinic for something to ease her pain."

I gave her ten *pesetas*? This morning? Yes, I did drop a coin into the cup of the beggar woman who sits in the alley. The one with the ragged shawl about her shoulders, her dirty blond hair spiked with purple glitter. Rubbing brown ointment on twisted legs. Not this lady who walks with the glide of the angels. One arm? One hand? And a grotesque fin?

This graceful pourer of wine for the multitude bares her crippled shoulder in my face. "See this," she says, "ghastly but it serves, for they toss me a brighter coin, tourists like you.

Her blue eyes bore into my soul. "Penance," she tells me. "To save us all, but you especially."

As we partake one of the twelve wants to know, "Where you from and where you going?"

And another with a wink asks, "Why a pretty young woman traveling alone?"

I cannot reply.

"We're for sure fearsome," they laugh. "But these old guys, they join us."

I look into the faces of the stone saints afloat in the slow circle of the candle beams. The one called Tomas hobbles over to a granite Virgin, puts her crown on his head.

"Looks good on me," he chortles.

"Belongs on her." His friends nod toward Our-Lady-of-the-one-Beautiful-Arm.

She takes my hand. "Come," she tells me. "You must go. The priests enter early for private devotion. They expect us to be gone to our places in the streets."

The great bells of the cathedral strike five as I insert the key in *Señora* Teresa's lock. She's standing there at the top of her steps, hands on her hips.

"I've been afraid for you," she says sharply. "The streets are not safe. Too many vagrants."

"I met them," I tell her. "They showed me the cathedral."

You're drunk," she says. "*¡Vente!* some chocolate."

On our way to the kitchen *Señora* pauses to cross herself before the little Virgin in the shrine by my door. In the half light of the morning the statue's robe conceals one arm. She extends the other.

MOM'S VIOLETS

One, two, three
What about ME?

My Mom's into African Violets. Each morning when Daddy leaves for his early rounds at the hospital they kiss good-bye next to her row of violets in the big bay of our kitchen window. After he's gone, in-between buzzing juice in the blender and stirring the oatmeal, Mom tends to her violets, pinching off a leaf here, snipping a weak stem there.

There's a bunch of us in our house: Mom, Daddy and me, plus Julie, my big sister who married Chuck. Their Charlie was born six months after the accident that killed Chuck. They live with us now so Julie can finish pre-med at the university. On a typical morning Charlie, his stinky diaper bumping along behind him, is the first down the stairs. Mom won't let him eat until he's cleaned up. Next thing Julie's in the kitchen telling him to shush his howling. About then I stagger in with my hair in disaster mode and my school pack loaded with everything I'll need to get through pre-calculus and Ms. Emory's advanced essay.

For my amazing Mom, pruning the little growths off her violets means making tough choices.

"Tough choices," she says, "lead to perfect flowers."

I've had to think a lot about choice lately. Picture me: blond, female, sixteen years, okay bod, C bra cups, cheerleader, decent student, all kinds of possibilities waiting in Technicolor just around the corner. Right! And I mean, do I or don't I come first?

At this point Daddy comes in from his study, ambles over to the stove where he dishes up his morning bowl of heart-happy oats. He gives me a shoulder squeeze just before he sits down at the table beside me.

"I'll be thinking of you today," he says and reaches out to hold my hand for a moment.

Mom and Daddy had Julie and me after Daddy finished medical school. I know the violet thing started some time around then, but Mom's never mentioned how or why. I make a private resolve to ask about them, but not now because Mom's digging for her keys and saying that we have to get going. To the clinic that is.

"Eight sharp," they said when I called to make the appointment.

On the way there I stare out the car window and try dodging the blues by forcing myself to list all the things I want to tell Vini this afternoon when I phone her for my assignments.

I blotch strawberry lip balm up to my nose when Mom swerves into the medical plaza parking lot. On the way into the building I stumble over a loose brick right below the doorstep so that I'm just regaining my balance when a clerk who'd come across as sweet, except her smile's in need of peroxide, holds the clinic door open for us.

"And how are we today?" she asks.

"Fine," I mouth at her, but my insides slosh like the grape *Jell-O* I snarfed last week when I couldn't keep anything else down. When I'm coming apart like I am now every word people say spears mega volts at me because I've made up my mind to do something whole gobs of people don't get with and I'm feeling deep pain. What if word gets out around school and every living soul flips jokes my direction in the cafeteria while I do a solo sweat-out at the back corner table by the gym doors?

Another lady, this one in a soft puffy sweater with cute pearl buttons, tells me her name is Betty. She puts a pitcher of water on the dressing room table beside me.

"We need a full bladder for the Ultrasound," she says. "It will move the intestines away from the uterus."

Mom pours six ounces into a plastic cup, gives it to me. My hands shake. Half of it ends up on the floor.

Betty hands me a key to a locker and one of those paper hospital gowns designed for an air-conditioned rear view.

"Everything off from here to there," she says waving one hand from my waist to the yucky mud-brown floor tiles under my feet.

"At the least they could use stickums or crayons or something to decorate this lame excuse for a cover-up," I say to Mom who's folding my clothes precisely and stacking them neatly on the locker shelf.

"Perhaps." Mom forces a smile out of some way-off private space, closes the locker and slips the key into her purse.

I shrug, then hand her the purple marker Betty's left on the counter top.

"Do something to make this thing I have on happy," I command.

Mom does violets.

"Why violets?" I ask.

There's no time for her to answer because a nurse's aide has me stand on the big scale in the corner by a stainless steel trash can, this institution's high-tech receptacle for tossed syringes, torn aspirin wrappers, and maybe even bloody gloves. I close my eyes when she moves the little lead weight on the scale over one more notch to the right.

"Ratchet down in the calorie count department," I mutter.

The aide nods like she's listened to that line before. Next she sticks my arm with a big needle which promptly loads up with a gallon of blood.

"Healthy. Lots of iron," the aide says with a smile.

My teeth begin to rattle.

Betty glides back into the room. All the tiny buttons on her pink sweater blink potty messages my direction.

"Red-alert in the bladder department," I moan.

But Ms. Pink Sweater encourages me to hold it just a bit longer so I have to do a maximum severe grip on my sphincter as we walk across the hall to a narrow room. At Betty's directive I hike myself up onto one of those high examination tables where doctors do their thing. After I'm settled, a little round lady named Rose applies gobs of warm gooey gel all over my lower tummy.

"Nice that it's warm," I say.

Rose talks as she works. "Sure, Sweetie. Used to be we had to use it cold. Now we microwave it into warm and thick and sticky for better contact between the abdominal wall and this little microphone. That way we get a clear echo."

A technician hustles in, all business. She runs the transducer thing back and forth, round and round on my stomach. It tickles and by this time my bladder's really set to burst, a bad combination, but I squeeze even harder down there and try to concentrate on what's happening.

The technician turns the video screen my way. "That little blob there. Mostly placenta. Eight and a half weeks," she says.

I take a half-grudging look at the screen.

The itsy thing that's stood everything in my life on its head is maybe one inch long. That teeny-tiny, one inch of possible baby is the cause of multiple nights pounding my pillow while my head mustered an entire squad of totally panicked versions of my life story.

Unbelievable!

The John call is screaming on emergency status. Betty hands me a paper cup. "Mid-stream in this," she orders. "After that you may get dressed. Take a mini break with your Mom? Remember, only a little juice or water for you. We'll see you back in an hour for the procedure."

We go to the deli across the street. I sip ice water through a yellow straw. A cup of peach yogurt for Mom who has big blue half moons under her eyes the way they get after she's spent a long night up with Charlie.

Mom looks at me hard. She reaches across the table to squeeze my hand. "You know," she says. "Dad and I had to go through this way back when he was finishing medical school."

Mom shreds her paper napkin bit by bit into a pile by her water glass as she tells me their story.

"It happened when Daddy was finishing medical school and money was so tight," she says. "We depended on my salary. We had been married for two years. At night we'd sit out on the flat roof of the little Philadelphia row house we shared with another couple and make all kinds of family plans. We thought two people couldn't be more in love, even if we were so poor that I added dried mint to our used tea bags to make them go further. I grew that mint on the house roof in old coffee cans. We were very careful, but then

I missed a period and a second one. Daddy cried when I came home with the news. He said he'd quit school. I refused to let him do that."

I look at her and it comes to me that abortions weren't even legal back then. They didn't have "day after" pills either. The pills that a couple of months ago I couldn't believe I needed to use.

"Did you have to go someplace far away?" I ask.

"We didn't have any money for that and I knew your father would stop school if I didn't act quickly. I'd heard all about the back-alley butchers who left women maimed for life. The whole idea of an abortion scared me.

Mom's voice came out a little trembly. Her stack of torn paper bits tumbled into the puddle ringing her water glass. I wanted to say, "It's all right. Don't say another word," but instead, "Did Daddy go with you?" slid slowly out.

"He did," she said. "We both needed that."

Mom told me her abortion routine was over quickly. "I rested for an hour afterwards," she said. "I drank some hot tea and they gave me pain pills. Finally, we went back home on the Spruce Street trolley. Your daddy wanted to buy me ten dozen roses, but all he could afford was an African violet with one tiny white flower."

African violet! My stomach does a long double flip.

"We've never told anyone." Mom's speaking softly and even more slowly than before. We're holding hands and wiping tears all at the same time.

"Does it hurt?" I want to know.

"Actually, the physical pain is not so bad," she says. "It's the tug at the heart that lingers."

She tells me this quietly, as if she's praying, only she's looking straight at me.

"Honey, it's plain hard to be a woman," she says softly. "Plain hard to know when to use your head and how to make sure your heart is big enough to make the right choice for yourself, for the child who could be, and for those close to you. That power to choose is what's scary about being a woman."

My Mom just called me a woman. Boom like that.

For a long minute we sit there saying nothing, but really connected in a deep woman way.

"Enough of this," Mom gives her hair a quick finger lift, puts on fresh lipstick.

"Come along," she says, picks up the bill, gets out her credit card, and pushes a generous tip under her plate.

I'm staring out the deli window. A big wind down out of the mountains tumbles the last of the fall's tired brown leaves into the gutter. Any minute now we'll have rain, and maybe the winter's first snow. There's a crowd now on the sidewalk in front of the clinic.

"I spot trouble," I tell her. "Something like the morals brigade."

Mom stands in front of the window, her hands on her hips and the set to her jaw Julie declares she gets when armoring up like Joan-of-Arc to lead her troops into battle.

Mom flings her purse over her shoulder. "Stand straight," she tells me, "walk right through them. Smile."

My mom marches out the door. I follow.

Outside, she pulls my arm through hers. Like the head referee at a big game, she waves a black pickup to a stop so we can cross in the middle of the street.

Suddenly we're surrounded. Everybody's yelling about killing babies. Some men elbow us with ugly, blown-up cartoons of half-formed creatures. A woman in an old black coat flips full color pictures of baby-in-utero in my face. She tries to stuff them into my jean pockets.

"Get your hands out of my pants," I yell.

There's lots of pushing and shoving, but Mom keeps on walking, her eyes fixed on the clinic door.

She's smiling and repeating, "No, thank you. No, thank you," and she's gripping my arm with both hands.

Sirens wail behind us. A powerful gust of icy rain pounds our backs, soaks the collars of our jackets, and destroys Mom's hair.

"Excuse us," Mom says to a man who's stretched out prone across the sidewalk.

He doesn't move. To get around him we make a wide detour through the wet grass.

A policewoman takes my arm.

"Come along," she orders as she guides us to the clinic door which opens just wide enough to let us enter.

"Calm down," Betty tells me, "and don't worry, this procedure will be over before you know it."

There's barely time to put my things back in the locker before a nurse bustles in with two pills and a tiny paper cup of water.

"For cramping during and after the procedure and to minimize bleeding," she explains.

A doctor in green scrubs nods recognition at Mom from the doorway, but I don't know him and he doesn't give me his name.

"Hey, it's me who's important here," I shout inside myself. "The key is me and what this will or will not do to the rest of my life."

Betty hands him my chart.

He reads it through, slowly once and then a second time.

Jeez, I think, he must be memorizing it.

"Looks good," he says to the chart.

The nurse motions me up onto another of those hard narrow tables.

From where I'm lying with a single pillow under my head and a thin sheet making for a bit of modesty, my only view is straight up at an oversized ceiling poster of an Hawaiian surfboarder cresting a huge blue wave.

While I'm dealing with waves, a nurse in full scrubs jabs my arm with another giant needle.

"This will help you to relax," she says.

The waves in the picture over my head start to move.

"They're going backwards," I tell her. My speech sounds slow, far away.

The nurse gives me a look that says she's heard about wrong-way waves before.

I close my eyes.

They have my legs spread wide now with my knees hanging over padded saddle-like supports. The doctor seats himself between them. There's a bright light shinning from his head.

The waves keep moving. I feel drowsy. I know it's the medicine.

The wave curls up and up. The doctor talks to me as he does a pelvic.

"I have to confirm the size of the uterus," he tells me, "and I need to hold the vagina open so I can see the cervix."

More white foamy things slide on the water. Mom's white violets whirl with the wave then fade into the blue ocean.

Betty squeezes my right hand.

Mom does the same on the left.

I murmur something about the foam looking like her violets. She pats my arm.

The doctor pokes some more. "And now, I'm inserting rods to dilate the cervix. Feeling crampy?" he asks. His voice floats far away like the violets.

"Yes, but okay," I mumble.

What I feel is the first level of cramps, then a second and then, Oh Wow, a third!

Actually, I'm miserable! At least I'm doing this with a pain killer. Poor Mom did it with almost nothing.

The row of little pearl buttons on Betty's fuzzy pink sweater gleams bigger and brighter and awfully whiter.

"It's over," she says. "Five minutes is all it takes."

"Gosh," I mutter, "that all?"

"I'll have to tell Daddy tonight that the hardest part is in the head," I tell Mom while I'm resting on the bed in the recovery room.

Mom looks at me. "What about the heart?" she asks.

"I guess I've not totally bought into the heart part yet," I tell her.

Mom runs her fingers through my hair which is still damp from the rain.

"Don't keep the feeling part of this down too long," she says.

Back home I collapse on the couch in the family room, pull the afghan up to my chin and lie there, eyes closed, absolutely motionless. Mom tiptoes about. The house is quiet, Charlie's down for his nap and Julie's gone out.

The whole scene from what happened at the crazy party where it all began through the action at the clinic today reruns in slow motion behind my eyes. And I'm standing in front of the entire production shouting over and over, "It's my life, my future, nobody else's!"

But Mom's white violets give this whole process another dimension, a deep inner heart place which is so tough it's totally, awesomely scary.

All-of-a-sudden, big hot tears squeeze out from beneath my eyelids and I'm shaking so the afghan tumbles into a pile on the floor.

I dig into my jeans' pocket for a tissue. One of those baby killer fliers the woman in front of the clinic waved in my face comes out along with it. The fine print runs in crazy lines across the page. Little red hearts dance around the blowup of a tiny creature in the middle.

Bingo. It's clear to me that what's in my heart connects, but in a very different way with that could-be-a-person-someday curled in the circle of bleeding hearts.

And right then Charlie's standing at the bottom of the stairs rubbing the sleepies out of his eyes with one hand, grasping the banister with the other.

"Big poop," he announces.

Mom grabs him. He howls for me.

With Charlie under one arm and a pile of clean laundry under the other, Mom looks in at me.

I've got the blown-up baby flier in my hand, tears running down my cheeks.

"Well?" she says.

Charlie wiggles free. "Poop," he grins.

"Okay, Tiger," I tell him and haul him back up the stairs. Mom follows, the laundry still tucked under one arm.

I push the diaper down into the neck of the diaper pail with one hand while I'm holding both Charlie's legs at the ankles with the other. He needs a complete scrub-up, followed by a cloud of talcum powder, a big squeezy hug and a kiss on the end of his round pug nose.

Charlie rides off on his blue tractor.

Mom's sitting in the big rocker still holding the laundry. There's a long line of gray roots marching through the jumble the wind made of her hair and there's mascara where blusher should highlight her cheekbones.

"Give it time to settle," she tells me.

I wave the flier with its tiny hearts in front of Mom's face. "For me this message totally misses the whole bigger heart of it," I tell her as I take the laundry she's still holding and stack it on the top of the dresser for Julie to put away.

Mom's looks right at me. "The larger heart, that's the center of it. That's where the hard choices are made," she says.

That evening Daddy's late for supper. One step in the door and he spots Mom standing beside the violets turning each pot toward its own best light.

Daddy takes Mom in his arms. They stand there for a long time, very quietly, like Julie and Charlie and I aren't even there.

Finally, she kisses him and they reach out to include us all in a huge family hug. After that Daddy goes back out to the car. He returns with a frilly pink

African violet. Mom sets it on the stand by their row of delicate white ones.

"For you," they tell me, "to celebrate your choice to go with the larger heart of it."

And this evening I'm doing my journal pages thinking larger hearts and poetry. Not the easy rhyming kind, but free verse which will let my amazing Mom's tough love from deep in the heart shine through. In my first draft the lines go like this:

For love, my Mom planted violets
    White ones with yellow centers and
        furry leaves
For love, my Mom tended them
    In their pots by the big bay window
For love, she snipped off the little stems
    To allow the strong green shoots to grow.

PURPLE JELLIES

Plastic shoes, everyone's doing them.

I do a solo run to the Big Apple for a day of transformation.

Catch the express at Princeton Junction.

Jersey fields speed by, sweet in country greens.

Nine now. Already hot!

Blazer wilts. Ankles swell. Feet sweat in shoes suddenly too tight.

Off at Penn Station.

Escalator up.

Step out. Pause, watching the crowd whirling, waiting in this cavern of a space.

Glance around. Would like to find that independent soul who pirouettes barefooted among the wingtips.

Where is she?

Take the long escalator up and out onto the street.

How about that other singular soul usually slouched in the bookstore doorway?

Not here today.

Individuals, these people of the street. Smart. Relaxing no doubt, each tucked into a private cubby on some solitary Atlantic beach.

Gloss over personal possibilities.

Orwell paperbacks stacked in a window. Black. White. Checkered.

Retro. Absolutely. Two decades ago everyone's reading Orwell in preparation for 1984. Things didn't work out, his definition of ideal community, lockstep in place.

Prediction failure?

Maybe.

Give the guy a break. Wrote in the forties. Hitler and all on his back. It's been sixty plus years.

And now, post the unthinkable planes crashed into twin towers, a new century.

Opportunity awaits!

Slip into a coffee place on Fifth; then spin up the avenue checking out window displays.

Scrutinize personal reflection. Something lacking. Definitely.

Careful!

Traffic's heavy. Cabs, beetle yellow. Trucks muscle red.

A long languorous limo slides by. Glass, one way. Color, cryptic maroon.

A bouncy blue Bug leads a streak-by of four wheeled alligators intent on prey.

This street, like a moat, both harbors danger and protects the postured parade of wooden mannequins in Lord and Taylor's cathedral windows just beyond the crosswalk.

Pedestrian signal flashes. Five seconds, four, three.

March, chin up right before the polished chrome teeth of those prehistoric four wheelers chomping for the next kill.

L & T's windowed wooden sylphs, long, lithe limbs, lathed to perfection, dazzle in smooth white cotton pants cropped at the ankle, dipped at the waist. And, all aglitter in the madcap morning sun: gold navel rings, gold toe rings, gold earrings.

Persistently the exaggerated bend of elongated wooden fingers points toward a polished bronze turnstile waiting to swirl the becharmed into this sanctuary of fashion's must-have parade.

Toward the community Congo of everybody's doing it, wearing it, being it.

I am swept from glare, asphalt and those vicious four-wheeled predators into a court of marble, of cut glass, of sweet perfume. An elegant retail spa designed to steam away inhibition's wrinkles.

Beside me now, a rumpled crowd.

As I am, restless.

Benevolently, L & T has foreseen the need to calm the strain of impending transition. There is coffee in silver pots, gold rimmed tiny cups, a maid starched in pale yellow, a red red rose in a very correct bud vase. We sip in silence, grateful for refreshment, for solitude before beginning this day's work of transformation.

At ten precisely the PA system plays the Star Spangled Anthem.

All rise.

Clerks gaze reverently at the polished floor.

Guards, at attention, stare into space.

We shoppers, pressing hand to heart, focus earnestly in the direction of the tiny flag anchored firmly on the main floor's information desk.

Song ends. Guards relax. Smiling, the maid takes our cups.

Group dismissed.

Mass break for the escalator.

Up to riots of striking scarlet, neon green, pinker pink. Tops in plushy peach, sea green, tea leaf brown. Up, up to robes in ranks of blues - - baby to sky to midnight.

Cheeks flush in the quest for that perfect something, that social admission ticket stamped, IN.

Round a corner. Sink into a chair. Look across the polished parquet.

There! Spotlighted. Tiered into a miniature ziggurat. Shoes. Yahoo yellow, opulent orange, roaring red and passionate purple plastic shoes. Jellied jewels. Decoration fit for the mass soul.

Perfectly awe-full. Purr-fectly right.

Trembling, I pick passionate purple.

Saleswoman murmurs, "Dear they mold to your feet."

Buyer kisses her fingers, "Mummmm!"

Elevator man nods approval.

Main floor perfume clerk smiles approval.

Doorman tips his hat, approval.

Dance out to Fifth in passionate purple plastic shoes.

Hot dog vendor whistles, "Lady those shoes!"

Flower vendor, pointing to his pair, chortles, "Green, you know for leaves and things."

Stride out. On course. Forward.

At the crossing one of those stretched limos shouts, "Lady mine are yellow. Watch where you're going."

Everyone has them.

Penn Station now. Escalators down. In unison all raise heads to call board. All rush in rhythm down stairs. All hop onto train. All sit precisely in seats. All read *The Times*. All hold tickets up for conductor's punch. The group protests a lone smoker.

Trainman shouts, "Junction."

Seat partner looks over, smiles. "Like your shoes. Seems everybody's wearing them. Orwell really missed the boat didn't he, all that black and white. My wife's got a pair in red."

www.ingramcontent.com/pod-product-compliance
Lightning Source LLC
Chambersburg PA
CBHW030427310726
48979CB00009B/1649/J

* 9 7 8 0 8 6 5 3 4 4 3 4 1 *